SHAGGED

ALEX WOLF

I don't like people.

I avoid them whenever possible.

They always want something from me whether it's money or attention.

My ten-figure net worth isn't the product of being what people would consider a "nice guy."

When I see something I want—I take it.

I've been called an asshole more times than I can count, and I don't care.

Caring about things makes you vulnerable, and vulnerable is the last thing I'll ever be.

Until Christina walks in and threatens the foundation of my life with her tight little body, sassy mouth, and soft curves.

She doesn't put up with my sh*t.

She makes me human.

I fight the attraction.

But, there's one problem...

I have to have her.

I *will* have her.

Publisher © Alex Wolf April 20, 2018
Cover Design: Lori Jackson
Editor: Stacey & Aaron Broadbent
Formatting: Alex Wolf

CHAPTER ONE

Matthew Spencer was a man who had it all.

He woke up to the sound of fake birds chirping and artificial sunrise creeping up his wall. It was a program on his phone, designed specifically for that purpose.

He ran a rough, calloused hand through his hair and sighed contentedly. His eyes blinked open, focusing on the golden sun that slowly climbed to his left.

Another beautiful day of being me.

The rich aroma of his morning coffee wafted into his nose and he sniffed, then rolled over in bed, feeling quite rested and rejuvenated. Matty knew his morning routine by heart. He would get up at his own leisure, have a cup of coffee, eat a healthy breakfast prepared by his personal chef and nutritionist, and then maybe he'd consider starting work. *Maybe.*

His phone switched on using the same system that

handled his alarm routine. It buzzed with an influx of text messages and missed calls.

Matty Spencer was a popular man. He was a loved man. But he was also a busy man, and he was not about to leap out of bed for anyone.

They knew his phone was off all night. If it was important, they could come to him. They didn't *need* his attention. They just wanted it.

Although being loved was a rewarding feeling, to Matty, it was also very tiring. He was not a machine, made to constantly please others. He was aware of how desperately they clung to him for his wealth and connections.

The phone lit up again and rattled against the night-stand. He sighed and tensed up. It was as if he were under attack.

He glanced at the phone and decided to scroll through. His mother and a couple of friends had tried to call him. The jingling-coins ringtone told him that he'd received a message from one of the countless gold-digging sluts on his booty-call list. He snickered at that.

They all thought he was unaware of their intentions. He laughed at how foolish they were, knowing that he could play people the way they tried to play him. For all the people he despised and had to be polite to, there were hundreds more willing to grovel at his feet. He knew it was wrong to enjoy this, but he didn't care. Why should he put up with all the responsibilities of being wealthy and popular if he couldn't enjoy the perks?

As his body acclimated to the day, he rose and scrolled through more of his messages. Thank God he kept separate phones, one personal and one business. He couldn't imagine digging through the pile of shit trying to find an important memo from a client or partner.

Good morning texts from countless numbers who didn't even have names attached to them came through like clockwork. Sexts from three different girls—two with pictures. He didn't ignore those.

A message from his mother consisted of three hundred emojis and a cat picture. A few were friends begging for handouts. And, of course, one girl throwing a hissy fit because he'd rejected her the previous night.

It wasn't his fault he wasn't always in the mood for her. Sometimes he wanted someone else.

If there was one thing that Matty Spencer knew, it was the fact that he was an asshole. He wasn't so deluded as to believe that everyone liked him, or that he couldn't try harder—that he shouldn't be better, but at the end of the day, he knew he didn't have to be. It was good enough to be a billionaire, have every girl he reached for, and to be respected and admired.

When he was younger, he'd often cared what others thought of him. He'd done everything he could to please them. It'd only taken being ripped off twice to realize that you couldn't be a pushover in this world. From then on, he'd lived only for himself. At thirty-one, that philosophy had yet to fail him.

He dropped his phone on the floor and walked to the window, pressing a button and watching the screen roll up. A beautiful view of the London skyline appeared in front of him. He nodded and smiled, pleased with the day, before wandering over to the other side of the room where his coffee would be ready.

He sipped it. Perfect aroma, perfect taste, and perfect temperature. Modern technology was a wonderful thing, coordinating his mornings for him. He streamlined everything in his life to suit his needs. And to think that he'd funded and co-developed all the programs which made his house run so seamlessly. No doubt his shower would be ready to begin, his chef would've just received the message to prepare his breakfast, and his maids received an alarm telling them his bed would need to be made. Most mornings he didn't even have to think actual thoughts until eleven or twelve. It was beautiful.

His business phone rang, interrupting his thoughts. A loud tone, immediately associated with one person. His secretary at his office. She knew not to contact him unless strictly necessary. Sighing, he called out to his robotic assistant on his phone. "Mia, answer call."

Emilia Hernandez's voice came through crystal clear as though she were standing next to him in the room. "Sorry to bother you, Mr. Spencer. I'm sure it's some misunderstanding, but—"

"It's fine. What is it?" He took another sip of his coffee.

"The partners from Watanabe Corp are here. The agenda does say you have a meeting with them."

"When? It's not on my planner." He scrolled through his daily tasks.

"About an hour ago. I tried to get hold of you, but it went straight to voicemail."

"Shit, I must have synced it with my personal one." Matty groaned. "I don't see any appointment listed."

"Well, they're in the office, and they're pretty angry. I can try and stall, but it's probably best if you get down here."

He groaned and straightened up. "Tell them my cat died this morning. I'm distraught. They'll buy it." Matty snickered to himself. Even the rich were idiots sometimes.

"Of course. Anything else?"

"Nope. Mia, end call."

As soon as the phone shut off, Matty said, "Mia, call Mr. Johannes. I need to rearrange some things."

He grabbed his clothes as Mia connected him.

This inconvenience perturbed Matty. He was a busy man—not a rushed-off-his-feet, nine-to-fiver. He didn't have to get up at six, and had no desire for a morning commute—but he was busy all the same. The thought of an eight-hour workday vexed him to no end. He'd carefully structured his life to avoid these types of circumstances, and his foolproof system had failed him.

He ran a vast company selling smart-home solutions, about to enter trade with one of the biggest app developers in the world, and his own system had let him down and caused him to be late.

"Yes, Mr. Spencer," said Mr. Johannes, as soon as he picked up. "How may I help you?"

Matty shrugged on his button-down and moved to the mirror, running a pre-warmed brush with a light layer of gel through his hair. "Is Terrence here? I'm running late for a meeting. I need a ride."

"Terrence has the day off, Mr. Spencer."

Matty's jaw clenched. He didn't enjoy inefficient conversations. When he made a statement, he expected a solution. Not a fact. "Well, who is on duty?"

He could practically feel Johannes wince on the other end of the line.

"Nobody, I'm afraid, Sir. There are no chauffeurs available until tomorrow."

Matty scrubbed a hand through his hair and thoroughly disheveled it. He swore under his breath and ran the comb through it again. "We're in London. I'm positive there is someone in this city that is capable of driving."

"Of course, Sir. I shall call in a new chauffeur immediately. We should have one by twelve."

"Twelve?" Matty groaned and his fingers tightened around the brush. "A fucking taxi would be faster than that. I needed to be at the office an hour and a half ago."

"I shall call Terrence and pay him triple to come to work right away. But that will nevertheless take at least forty minutes. Considering your present predicament, a taxi may be the fastest option."

Matty paused.

Could he wait for a taxi? Or for Terrence to arrive? No. This deal was important. Not vital, but important. It would help his company. It would make an exorbitant amount of money. Fuck it, he'd drive himself. "I'm driving. Leave the keys to the Lambo by the front door."

"Of course, Sir. Anything else before I attend to that?"

"Nothing."

"Very well, Sir."

Matty took a quick glance in the mirror, flew down the hall, and out the front door. Standing in the street, holding his keys, he glanced around. It didn't take a genius to realize something was seriously wrong.

His car was gone. Nowhere to be found. "Goddamn it!" He looked up and down the street once more. Had someone moved it? Had he accidentally stopped it down the road, in front of a neighbor's house?

No such thing. His eyes landed on a bright yellow sign.

A no parking zone? Seriously? And they hadn't even knocked on his door to let them know they were towing away a fucking Lamborghini?

This wasn't some shitty little suburb or quaint country town. This was an area entirely inhabited by the elite, living in urban mansions worth tens of millions of pounds. Which councilor with a stick up his ass had approved a no parking zone?

Matty took a deep breath. It would be fine. He had plenty of other cars. He'd just waste another minute, go inside, and get one.

The limo would be too ostentatious, but he had a Ferrari that would be quick and look nice and sleek as it pulled into his private garage beneath the building.

He folded himself inside the low-lying vehicle and backed out. At last, on the road. He flew around a few corners, the engine a low growl. Matty wondered how other people did this every day. He *loved* driving. Adored it. How could you not when you had a car that was so sleek, powerful, and beautiful? But on this busy, smoggy road? Surrounded by these imbeciles? It was like sitting on a golden throne in the pits of Hell. Torture from a luxurious seat was still torture.

A blue light flashed behind him and left him with a sinking sensation. *Please let it be an ambulance.*

Police.

Shitfuck.

He pulled over and rolled his window down as the officer approached from behind. "I don't have fucking time for this."

"I can see that. It's why you're getting a speeding ticket." The officer strolled up next to the window.

"A ticket? Are you not aware who I am?" Had he even broken the law? He'd been in a rush, but he hadn't thought he was speeding.

"Someone who can afford a ticket, Sir. Let's not make it into something worse."

Matty nodded and stared at the whites of his knuckles as he gripped the wheel. "Sure, just—let me have it, and I'll be on my way."

With the ticket firmly wedged in his pocket, he drove swiftly, but not too swiftly, to his office building, parked, and tried to balance the urgency of the situation with the need to look professional, and composed. It wasn't like a few more minutes would make much of a difference.

I need to sort my life out.

He walked up to the desk where Emilia waited with a sympathetic smile, her warm brown eyes and full face fell somewhere between motherly and matronly.

"Can you call and see if there is a human we can hire to organize things? A babysitter for adults, perhaps?" Matty asked.

"Can Mia not handle things, Sir?"

Matty shook his head. "I'm afraid not."

"I was just thinking of the company image."

Matty nodded. "Understood." He paused and let out an exasperated sigh. "I need you to keep quiet about this for that very reason. But, I need an actual person to tell me where the fuck I'm going wrong."

Emilia nodded and smiled. "I'll look into it while you attend the meeting, Sir."

"You're a star." Matty breathed a sigh of relief. Now, all he needed to do was survive this bloody meeting.

————

Despite the initial setback, he managed to appease the Watanabe partners, and it looked as though a long-term relationship between their companies would be beneficial enough for them to overlook the morning's near disaster. They seemed to buy the cat story, which amused Matty to no end. However, the adrenaline quickly settled, and the need for a fresh coffee arose as he waved goodbye from the hallway.

The elevator doors slid closed and he turned around to face Emilia. "Any luck then?"

"Well, I did remember that your friend, Mr. Arvin, suggested a PA last time he was here. *And* that you laughed at him. But I thought maybe you would have reconsidered, so I contacted him and asked for her name." She handed him a small appointment card.

"Not storing it on Mia this time?"

Emilia shook her head. "Not because of that. I thought if someone were to remotely access your planner they might—"

"Smart move. Maybe you could organize my life for me instead?"

Emilia shook her head once more. "Sorry, Sir. I only really handle times and dates, names and places. And from what Mr. Arvin said, Ms. Smith is a little more thorough."

"She will be here tomorrow?" Matty twirled the card between his fingers thoughtfully. All it had was a name, a phone number, and a time scribbled on it. "Five p.m.?"

"*Today* at five p.m., Sir. I said it was a matter of urgency, but to be discrete. She will see you at your home."

Matty nodded. "Perfect. I suppose I'd better head back. Unless there are any other appointments I'm unaware of?"

"None, Sir." Emilia stared anywhere but at Matty, avoiding eye contact.

"Hey."

Her eyes moved up and met his.

"I don't blame you for any of this, just so you know. You're the warden of this nuthouse, but I won't hold you responsible for the meltdowns."

Matty didn't enjoy being bothered with trivial nonsense, and it usually perturbed him to no end. But, he'd learned long ago, not to piss off the help. Emilia was a valuable asset to him, and a loyal one at that. It served him well to keep her happy.

His company's automated system had fucked up his day for the last time, though. It was time to bring in a professional human, and let them do the job.

"Grateful to hear that, Sir. Oh, and Mr. Arvin said, please pardon my language but these were his exact words: 'Look out, she knows what she's doing and she's great, but she can be a total bitch.'" Emilia smiled as professionally as always.

Matty nodded. "I'll bear that in mind."

"Is there anything else, Sir?"

"No, that'll be all. Thank you."

CHAPTER TWO

A pproaching Matthew Spencer's house, Christina Smith knew she was dealing with a very wealthy client. The mansion looked new and extravagant, like it'd been ripped out of Hollywood and dropped in the middle of a London suburb.

Sandy walls framed the place, and the gate was wide enough to fit a tank through. The gardens were full of exotic plants, dotting the greenery with splatters of reds, pinks, yellows, and blues. It was also the only garden on the street which hadn't been carefully manicured that morning. Couldn't he afford to pay someone to come landscape the house?

He'd called for her to come at once. Seemed more likely it was a breakdown in communication. He definitely needed her services if he couldn't even keep his lawn mowed.

She walked up to the front gate and noticed that the intercom had a two-way video option.

Christina flipped open a mirror and made sure that her hair was still firmly tied back, and her makeup was clean and professional. The more money these guys had, the more perfection they demanded. When she'd first started, she'd assumed her work would speak for itself. That'd been a mistake.

Her skin had to be flawless, her lips cherry red, and the lines of her makeup sharp. Her wavy brown hair had to be pulled and twisted until there wasn't a single stray hair sticking out. Her dress was tailored, dry cleaned, pressed, and she wore perfume that was two hundred pounds an ounce.

If she was not perfectly dressed and on point, how could they trust her to organize everything for them?

Reassured that she looked okay, she pressed the button on the intercom. It came to life, and an older man in a dark suit stared back at her on the screen. "Good afternoon, please state your business."

"Umm, I'm Ms. Smith. I have an appointment with Mr. Spencer. Five o'clock. I'm a few minutes early."

"Very well. Do come in."

There were no subtle options for entering the estate. Not unless you were a servant, it seemed. Everyone was forced to go through the main entrance.

The gates creaked open slowly with a slight squeak. She could see the older man already waiting at the door. She was used to places like this and knew many of the people in these houses actually lived paycheck to paycheck and were up to their eyes in debt. By now, she'd learned to have a nose for money. And judging by what she'd seen so far, this guy—like his friend Mr. Arvin—was loaded.

There were little signs of extravagant wealth woven through the place. There were also many signs that these things were seriously neglected. A unique sculpture sat near the porch. It didn't look like it'd been cleaned anytime recently. Many of the exotic plants were beginning to wilt without any reason for it. A solid gold knocker hung on the door. It was just for looks. Nobody would ever use a damn knocker. Whoever she was helping was someone that never thought before buying.

No wonder he needed her help.

The older gentleman welcomed her in, guided her to a main living area and asked her to wait there for Mr. Spencer. She walked around the room, scoping it out. The inside was as much of a mess as the outside.

She spotted a pile of unopened mail on the table by the window. An overdue bill was up on the mantlepiece when she strolled over. A dirty coat was out in the hallway, on the floor. All normal things in a normal house, but very out of place in a mansion with a ton of employees to keep the place running. Finally, she sat down in one of the chairs and waited.

"Good afternoon, you must be Ms. Smith?" A rich, baritone voice came from the hallway the second she'd taken a seat.

She whipped around to face the man. "Yes, Sir. Are you Mr. Spencer?" It couldn't be him. This guy was too young to have this kind of money.

"I am." He walked over to the chair across from her but stood instead of sitting down.

"It's nice to meet you." She stood and held out a hand.

He waved her off without shaking. "Do sit back down."

It was always hard to tell how these wealthy people wanted her to act. Even social interactions were like games to them. They always had to be in control. They always treated employees like they were less than them and showed off their power any chance they got. Most of the time, it was telling her to do the opposite of whatever she was doing. But she always played along. It didn't hurt anybody. She sat down and waited for him to explain why she was there.

Her game was thrown off for a second, and she had to regain her composure. She wasn't used to having clients that didn't have gray hair. He was also one of the tallest, strongest looking men she'd ever seen. Breathing became difficult when she got a good look at him. He could've easily been a movie star or a musician. In fact, he probably was. She just hadn't recognized him because she didn't pay attention to celebrities and gossip magazines. It was rare for someone under sixty to live in a place like this, and Mr. Spencer looked like he was pushing thirty at the most.

"I'm sure you get asked this a lot, but what is it exactly that you do?" He walked around her chair and then over to the window, where he shuffled through the letters, clearly not sure where to begin.

The man didn't even know why he was hiring her. That wasn't surprising. "You should put them into separate piles for bills, personal, circulars, and business. Then work through them by date."

He glanced at her. "I see."

"That's what I do. I show you how to manage your home. I make sure you have all the staff you need, line up all your schedules. Help you get more organized."

"Like one of those automated solutions?"

"No way. Those things are a disaster. The technology isn't there yet. Unlike a computer, I can actually reason and make decisions on the spot, as opposed to depending on how someone coded a computer." She thought for some kind of analogy she could use. "I guess you could think of me as a sort of modern Victorian housekeeper, or a personal business manager."

"I'm still none the wiser." His words had an edge to them, like maybe she'd offended him somehow. "But I suppose it's worth a chance." He put the letters down and stalked back over to her chair. "Do you want me to explain the problems to you?" Mr. Spencer sat down in front of her.

She shook her head. "If you knew the problems, you would've solved them by now."

He let out an exasperated sigh. "I'm pretty sure I know what's wrong with my own house."

"Sorry for being forward, but you know the consequences of the problems, not the problems themselves. It's like being sick. Everyone knows their symptoms, but they still go to a doctor to be diagnosed and treated. I'm here to diagnose your life and prescribe a treatment for it."

"That makes more sense to me. You're analyzing the

situation. At the end, would my life be cured of its ailment?"

"I've never left a patient ill." She paused with a slight smile. "Now, sometimes clients stop treating their condition and symptoms return, but if you follow my plan, you shouldn't have to see me again."

"Are you sure that none of your clients let the symptoms return purposefully?" His eyes raked down to her heels and back up.

Christina nodded. She knew exactly what he meant. "I'm sure it happens. That's up to them."

"You're prepared to start immediately?"

She nodded. "Absolutely."

"Great. Once you've been shown around just do whatever it is you do. And if you need anything, don't hesitate to ask the other members of the staff."

"Will do. Thank you, Mr. Spencer." And just like that, she had a new job.

"One last thing."

"Sir?"

His voice lowered. "I'm not sure how much Emilia told you about my business, but, we need to keep this all *very* quiet."

"Your secretary didn't tell me anything about what you do."

"I'm actually the owner of Mia, the smart-house."

She realized why he was frustrated a few moments before. "Umm, you designed Mia?"

"In a way. Not on my own, obviously, but yeah." He shrugged.

"Sorry for what I said earlier." Shit, that could've cost her the job.

He shook his head. "No. Between you and me, Mia's a disaster."

It all made sense at once. The owner of a company that sold smart-home solutions was living in complete disarray. He needed a human professional to fix his personal life. No wonder he was so evasive and probably embarrassed. And he was so desperate he'd made an appointment with her.

She smiled. "No worries. We can fix this."

"I bloody well hope so. Let's have a tour of the house."

She stood up and his eyes burned through her. He may not have noticed her figure before, but he definitely did now. It didn't take a genius to realize he was checking her out. And why wouldn't he? She was petite, with perfect, full curves that had been squeezed into a tailored dress—along with impeccable hair and makeup. Christina knew most men thought she was hot. Her male clients all looked at her the same way.

It was definitely clear that Matthew Spencer liked her. Everything about him changed as they walked from room to room. The way he carried himself, his tone of voice. Not to mention the fact that he was personally showing her around.

His hand fell on the small of her back as he guided

her to the next room. She figured he was also a man who didn't know what it was like to be rejected. This could either be fun or torture. She wasn't sure. But there was no way she would reciprocate.

She had a personal rule of not sleeping with clients, and her work made dating impossible. She spent weeks at a time living in strange men's houses, flying around the world to fix their personal lives. She was fortunate Mr. Spencer lived in the same city as her. She was always busy. And she had to be a cold bitch to get the respect she deserved. Otherwise, these men would walk all over her.

Trying to ignore the way he placed his hand on her back, she took in her surroundings.

Everything was perfectly clean, but out of place. Lights were on in rooms with large, bright windows, and turned off in dark hallways. Shit was strewn over tables and chairs, as though someone had set it down and then forgotten it was there. As he walked, Mr. Spencer explained all his problems. Missed appointments, employees not coming in on the right days, contractors not being called in for repairs, or none of them were coordinated right.

He was just spending, spending, spending, like a boy with his father's credit card. Every time something went wrong, he threw money at it until it went away. A rough calculation told her he was spending about five times more money than he should.

She'd worked for men with the same issues, but Matty Spencer was taking it to the extreme. The place looked like it'd been decorated by a frat boy. At least the place wasn't too cluttered, and he had servants to keep the place clean, but, the decorating was all nudes and edgy pop art, or expensive cars—classical sculptures, and original prints from famous artists. The aesthetic was what she would expect in a Harvard dorm room.

From the sound of it, the rest of his life went the same. He'd see something he wanted to do, and he would just go and do it. He'd just whip out the credit card at anything he wanted to buy. Anyone else would've been in trouble by now, but not Mr. Spencer. She figured he'd coasted through life on a combination of wealth and quick wit, and only now was he starting to feel the effect of it.

"You like the décor?" He smiled as he caught her staring at a large sculpture of a naked woman on a horse.

She nodded and faked a smile. "You have unique taste." She definitely had an opinion, but she wasn't there to improve his decorating skills.

Despite his atrocious sense of style, she couldn't help but be jealous. She made a decent living, but she'd never earn a fraction of what he spent in a year. She was desperately saving for a dream house back in Kentucky, for her father. She lived completely frugal. Only spent money on absolute needs and items she had to have for work. He could probably buy that modest home with his weekly paycheck. She couldn't imagine living some-where like this.

It was one of the perks of the job, though, living vicariously through her clients. She could enjoy beautiful houses during the day, and at night when she traveled.

Many of her clients had guest houses and didn't want to foot the bill for her to stay in a hotel.

Even with her local clients, she could usually get away with working a few hours every morning and then kicking back for the day. She was that good. Then she could sit back and enjoy expensive wine and whatever entertainment the home offered.

It would be a few weeks before she could do that here, though. This guy needed a lot of work. And the work always came first.

CHAPTER THREE

*F*uck me!

Christina was one of the hottest—no, *the* hottest woman Matty had ever seen. In all his years of dating models, actresses, even porn stars, he'd never seen a woman so perfectly proportioned with her hourglass frame. She was sensual in every movement. She was— exactly his type. He never even thought he had a type before, other than "hot", but looking at her, he knew Christina was it.

Every little thing about her was breathtaking. She had brunette hair and sharp brown eyes. The way her tailored dress hugged her figure, clinging to her firm hips and tight waist. The sharpness of the painted lines on her face, the boldness of her lips, the way her eyeliner drew you into a mesmerizing gaze. The way she masterfully strode in skyscraper heels. Stilettos so tall that no woman should be able to get away with wearing them, yet somehow clinical and stern like the rest of her. Heels that took her from a petite Hispanic woman to a powerful goddess who could look men of his stature in the eye without needing to peer up like a child.

Normally he would mock or chastise women like her. She was cold. She was collected—a professional. She embraced her femininity only in as much as to announce her sex, and rejected every hint of softness, fragility, or humility foisted upon her. She was a woman, but a clean-slate, aseptic, robotic woman. All the female and none of the feminine. All the woman and none of the human. But goddamn, she wore it well.

Her look inspired confidence in him. On the one hand, he knew it was carefully crafted for that exact purpose. But on the other hand, any woman who could put herself together so perfectly, so sharply for an interview, and then hold that look, that character together— she was a walking advertisement for her own composure and order. And composure and order were precisely what he wanted to buy from her. Her presence in his home would be a pleasant little perk, of course. But she had a job to do first and foremost.

"I need you to start work as soon as possible." He guided her into his office. "I'm ashamed to admit, but everywhere I look I see nothing but disorder. This needs correcting. It's humiliating for a man in my position, in my industry, to be living in such disarray. If someone were to notice, the whole premise of my company may be called into question."

Christina made eye contact.

He could see the look in her eye, judging him, probably wondering why he was creating these products if he knew nothing about them.

"I can start today. If that's what you want."

He studied her for another moment. How could she talk without a hint of emotion on her face? Was she even a woman at all? Perhaps she really was a robot?

He wondered what shaped her and molded her into the way she was. Perhaps she grew up in an emotionless environment, or some trauma trained her to hide all her feelings. It didn't matter, though. He would hire her. She would whip the place into shape, and he'd go on living the way in which he was accustomed.

"I would like you to start immediately. I have a backlog of four weeks of paper letters. I hate them. I prefer emails and video calls. So they're completely unread. You can go through and organize them so I can manage them in the future."

"You know what I cost, right?" She raised an eyebrow.

"Haven't a clue."

She sighed. "It is nine hundred poun—"

"Don't care." He brushed her off with a flippant hand. "Just bill my secretary. No, my housekeeper. I can't have you connected to work."

Her face canted to the side. "You don't even need to think about the price?"

Matty stared at her, confusion written all over his face. "I don't care if it's nine hundred pounds a day, or an hour. Just send the bill." Surely, she was not so dense as to think he needed to budget.

"Mr. Spencer, this is the sort of attitude that got you

in this position. How you got by in life until now is beyond me."

Matty smirked. "These amounts aren't material enough to warrant close attention. Thank you for the concern, though."

"Well, one day when the money runs out. You'll be glad you hired me."

She began collecting the piles of papers and letters from the various shelves, open filing cabinets, and low tables around the room. He watched, wondering how she got by so far in her job with her snarky attitude. Usually, it took a few weeks for someone to hate him. This was a new record.

He fussed with his shirt cuff and watched her work. "Is the attitude part of the service or complimentary?"

"What do you mean? Am I supposed to call you 'sir'?"

"Well, you are my employee now."

Christina shook her head. "You hired me, but I'm not your servant, or an employee. I'll call you Mr. Spencer."

"Does this bluntness earn you many repeat customers? I don't recall asking for this attitude to be a part of the contract." He sat down on the edge of the coffee table, completely amused.

"If you had to work with children every day, your question would answer itself. I work with a lot of men in your position. I know how I *need* to speak to you."

Did she just compare me to a bloody child?

He knew for a fact he was at least five, maybe even ten years older than her. She couldn't be but what?

Twenty-five? This was new. He couldn't figure out if he should laugh or become angry.

Matty scoffed. "You know, I'm not sure I've ever been spoken to like this, requested or not."

"I said need, not want." She moved the stack of letters and papers onto the desk. "Nobody *wants* to be told the truth. But it's what my clients need. If I soften my words, trying not to offend anyone, then clients only hear what they want, and they ignore the actual message. Suggesting and implying things isn't good enough." She flashed him a clearly fake smile.

"It's more ladylike," Matty said. "Saying things so bluntly is not ladylike at all."

"I'm not a lady. I'm here to get results." She didn't even look up from the papers she was shuffling around to get just right. "Ahh, better." She sat down at the desk and began scrutinizing the letters.

He ought to be angry with her, fire her immediately. In all regards, he should probably hate her. She was everything he hated in a woman.

Yet somehow, every one of her actions drew him more to her, like some kind of addiction. Normally, he liked his women passive, submissive, sweet and girly. But not Christina. She was—different. Perhaps that's why he currently enjoyed her company.

She lightly pressed the pen to her plump lips as she pored over a sheet, tapping her mouth gently in the manner of someone who used to chew pencils in school, but had since learned not to.

Drawing in a sharp breath, he realized that a heat

stirred inside him. He needed a drink. Something stiff to ease his mind and prevent additional stiffness.

"Care for a brandy?" He moved toward the cabinet.

"I don't drink on the job. I have to stay focused to give you the best work possible."

Matty shrugged with a grin. "I've never found a little sip at work to do any harm." He slowly selected one of the three aged brandies from his vast liquor cabinet. Christina stared at him as if he were an animal who should spend more time organizing the post than choosing a drink.

"Maybe that's why you had to call me."

He wanted to reply but could not think of anything. Damn, she had a sharp wit for a young woman. And an equally quick tongue. She was like the mind of a no-nonsense matron in the body of an American fairytale creature. Where was she from, anyway? His guess was South America. He didn't know much about the culture there. Maybe this was normal. It was a delightful challenge. How had she wound up crunching numbers and sorting post for anyone? Sure, it was better to be doing such menial tasks for a man like him, but he knew so many talent scouts who would whisk her off her feet in a heartbeat. How had she remained so undetected?

"I'm amazed a beautiful woman like yourself, working in this part of the country, is not something like a model, or an actress." He poured himself a drink.

"There are plenty of beautiful women who work in business."

Matty shook his head. "I've never, in my entire life, seen a woman as pretty as you who does not make a living off her looks. Especially not an unmarried woman. Do you not want to be a model? To be famous?"

Christina shook her head. "Nope."

"Too good for it? Too smart to make money off your looks?"

"Nope. Many models are smart. I know one or two myself."

"Did a model break your heart? Is that why you chose your current line of work?" He was genuinely baffled and couldn't help himself trying to break through her cold exterior. She was this attractive and knew models and had no desire of becoming one?

She paused her current task to stare up at him. "Beauty fades, sensuality expires. Being good at business doesn't." She stared up at him. "An intelligent model who knows how to play the system and become a recruiter might be able to make a living off it for her entire life. But I'm not good at that. Some of *us* would rather do what we're good at, instead of doing something we find fun."

That last bit was definitely another jab at him. Tommy Arvin hadn't been wrong. This woman *was* a total bitch. How she could treat her employer this way was beyond him. If she were anyone else he would have kicked her out, or started placing higher demands on her already. But he just smirked and sipped his brandy as she worked. He would *not* give in first.

Why did he like her so much? That was the issue that troubled him the most. She was precisely the sort of woman he avoided like the plague. The sort of woman he scoffed at, and who his friends would suggest suffered from lack of sexual activity. It was as though she had heard that men like feisty girls and decided, "Hey, that's cute, now let me show you how it's done." This was just pure cruelty.

But simultaneously, it was kind of nice. Her cruelty excited him, made him yearn for her even more. Despite being his social subordinate and an employee, she was somehow standing above him, on a pedestal. And he wanted to knock it out from under her, and show her who really was the boss.

Christina Smith was sort of an enigma. He should not like her. But he did. He wanted to break her down, to control her, to possess her mind, heart, and body. She was a challenge. And he was more than prepared to rise and meet her defiance.

"Perhaps I ought to make you a model. I cannot believe that any woman has at no point desired to be famous and admired for her beauty."

"I didn't say I never imagined being a model, or an actress, or a singer. But many people are afraid of blood and dream about being doctors, and a lot of people fear flying, and dream of being a pilot."

He shook his head. "Are you saying you wouldn't make a good model? You don't strike me as someone with such low confidence, but I suppose it's a possibility. Or do you mean to say that you fear failure? That would be odd for a businesswoman—"

She paused and put the papers down.

Matty came alive on the inside. Had he finally cut to her core? Put a chink in her armor?

"What I mean is that a dream is not necessarily connected to the reality of the world. What little girls picture when they dream of modeling isn't reality. Dreams aren't real. They don't come true. To put it bluntly, they're a waste of time."

That was one of the saddest things he'd ever heard anyone say. He actually pitied her in that instant. Everyone had dreams. Even he had things he aspired to do someday, that were beyond his reach. No matter how much money you had, there was always something you didn't have the time, the energy, or the connections to do. And he had an entire life plan mapped out to achieve his dreams.

"So, you gave up on all of your dreams? Just like that?"

She shook her head. "They're not my dreams anymore. I know how the world works, and I don't have what it takes to succeed in that environment."

"I have the means to make sure that you could succeed. And you most certainly have the beauty."

Why was he doing this? He was under no obligation to help her out. But he felt a dual impulse. On one hand he wanted to help her, and on the other to get her under his thumb—which motivated him to offer her everything he had at his disposal.

She glanced over at him. "Are you a model?"

He shook his head. "I know a few directors of agencies, and I've dated enough models in the past. I'm sure they'd be able to help you."

"Maybe we should just stick to what we know best." She held up the disheveled papers with a curt smile.

CHAPTER FOUR

Christina sighed and shook her head as she looked through the papers. There was something wrong with his head. How could he be so hung up on ideals, or dreams, or the fantasy world that everyone else left behind at fifteen? A modeling career? Just because she was attractive? He was insane.

The man was thirty-one for fuck's sake, and he didn't have an adult bone in his body. She'd done her homework. How had his company even survived his leadership? She knew he'd inherited it from his father, but he'd also owned it long enough that it should've fallen apart by now.

Amazingly, it was a success. Either a miracle had occurred, or there was something more to the guy than fast cars, models, and having more money than sense. What she'd seen didn't match up with her research, though.

"What do you plan on doing with your life?"

She rolled her eyes. He was still at it. Why was he even still there? He was nothing but a distraction.

His question jolted her out of her thoughts. She had to stifle a laugh. It was so cheesy. This asshole, of all people, was asking *her* what she planned on doing with her life? Why was it that rich men always assumed their lives were perfect just because they had money? Like she was floating around aimlessly, just begging for a man to save her because she didn't live in a mansion?

She made a show of holding her hands out at the now neatly-stacked pile of bills. "Isn't it obvious?"

"But where do you see it going?"

Christina shrugged. "Where do you see *your* life going?" She loved doing this. Throwing these apparently philosophical questions back at these rich pricks and watching them struggle to find meaning in their existence.

"I don't know. I'd like to someday be able to paint, I suppose, but there isn't much time for that right now."

Her eyes widened at his answer. She hadn't seen that coming. "Did you just, umm, admit that you don't know?" This was not how the conversation usually went. Normally they stuck to their guns and made a case that they were the most valuable person alive.

He nodded. "That's why I asked you. You seem pretty confident you have it all figured out."

She laughed. "Well, I don't. But I have a house I'm saving up for."

"That seemed like a genuine laugh. Be careful. You might injure yourself." Matty smirked.

Her face heated. Not only at his sarcasm, but at the

fact she was smiling. She forced her lips back down into a neutral position. He made her nervous, and he shouldn't. He was just a man. But fuck, he was a gorgeous one. She couldn't find a way around that fact.

His smile grew wider as if he could read her thoughts. "Is happiness against the rules?"

"I've learned that if I smile at a male client, they make it out to be more than it is."

He shrugged. "But that was a genuine smile, not a polite one. So it *was* more than it is. So why not let it happen?"

Was this whole conversation some kind of competition for him? What was it with men? It was a smile, Jesus.

Fine. He could play his little immature game. It wasn't like it mattered. She showed him an obviously fake smile. "Okay. I'll smile at work. I just have one condition."

"Which is?"

"That you leave the room. So I can get my work done in peace."

His lips mashed into a fine line, and his face paled. "Tommy is right. You are a bloody bitch."

She nodded, and her smile widened farther. "You got that right."

At first, fear came over her for some reason. She might lose him as a client for that. He might call security, or toss his expensive brandy at her. It wouldn't be the first time it'd happened. Wealthy, powerful men didn't always take kindly to rejection. They usually didn't appreciate the snark either. But if that was what she had to do to be treated professionally, then that's how it would be. Her dreams and personal life weren't his concern. She was hired to do a job, and he should let her do it.

Relief washed over her when he walked out of the room and left. He shouldn't insist on looming over her shoulder anyway. Nobody could work that way.

Back when she worked for a variety of clients, she hadn't experienced the same problems. Men with less money didn't seem to think they were entitled to her body or her personal life. They just appreciated the work she was doing for them, most of the time. The more money the man had, the less care he took with it, and the more likely he was to assume her job was pointless.

Egomaniacs. That's what they were.

Of course, they were the ones who suffered when they didn't listen to her, or when they fired her before she could do her job. But she personally made sure they didn't get away with that kind of behavior. She didn't let them, and she wouldn't, ever. Were other women allowing themselves to be treated like doormats? Or were these guys just so wealthy that the odd sexual harassment settlement didn't scare it out of them?

Normally, the clear signs of this type of thing had her avoiding the client whenever possible. A little bad behavior, a little entitlement, and she despised him immediately. Matty Spencer should be the same.

But for some reason, she still wanted to talk to him. To impress him. It was the strangest feeling. Even after all the banter, she felt compelled to do a good job for him. She wanted to show him what she was worth. There was something about him that set him apart, made him interesting to her.

She couldn't put a finger on it. Maybe it was the painting dream of his. Or his interest in her dreams. Maybe it was the fact he *had* actually admitted he didn't know what he was doing, and that the situation could be embarrassing for him. Maybe it was just pure magnetism. His blatant advances excited her in a way she hadn't felt in a long time, if ever. His cockiness was sexy. His mystery was thrilling. She wanted to slap herself.

No.

She couldn't let herself think about a client this way. She needed to work. Get her shit together. Not sit around fantasizing about her employer like a horny schoolgirl.

Perhaps it was because he was younger than her typical client. Hotter. So self-assured, despite his undeniable incompetence. She spent so much time working for pompous, dirty, old men, that someone like Matthew Spencer was a bit refreshing. At least he was nice to look at, slightly more in touch with reality, and managed to avoid really slimy behavior. It wasn't like he'd touched her, ogled her, or made glaring advances. He was an asshole and not all that bright, but he stood head and shoulders above her usual clientele.

But, no matter how much she reassured herself of all this, she found herself unable to concentrate on the work in front of her. She wondered why she could still feel his hand burning hot against her lower back where he'd guided her from room to room.

She had to pull herself together. Forget Matty Spencer and his gorgeous, broody eyes. That was all there was to it. She had a crush on her employer. It wasn't a big deal. He was handsome and rich and powerful. Of course she had a crush.

A silly infatuation wasn't valid grounds to ruin her career. She pored over the papers and began swiftly sorting through them without him in the room. *Much better.* Besides, how could she possibly think of sleeping with a man who couldn't even pay his bills on time? There was wealthy, and then there was just unbelievably irresponsible. If someone had a pile of money they didn't respect, it would soon be gone. It would drive her crazy being romantically involved with someone that careless.

Speaking of not lasting long, Matty walked back in and stared at her as she carried on working.

She rolled her eyes where he couldn't see.

The man refused to give up. All she wanted to do was get her job done. It seemed he was going to be one of *those* clients. But, she couldn't bring herself to tell him to leave again. She couldn't move to another room. Her feet were like concrete bricks.

She enjoyed him being there. It was almost soothing.

She decided she would just sit and work, not talk to him, and hope that he would take the hint and walk out. No such luck.

"How's it going?" Did he micromanage his employees at his business this way? Was he constantly walking into their offices to check up on them?

She refused to look up. "I'm a miracle worker, but

not even I'm that fast. It's been five minutes." She let out a sigh that was much heavier than she'd expected, like she'd been holding in a breath.

"You're very quiet." Matty walked to the liquor cabinet again. "You sure it's going okay?"

She couldn't help but watch as he moved over and poured himself another brandy. Was he an alcoholic? It was still the middle of the day.

She couldn't help but notice his impressive figure as he walked through the room in his suit. Whether he was an idiot or not, he definitely had that going for him. Was he doing it on purpose? Coming in the room just to torture her? She thought he'd made it pretty clear that he liked her, but maybe he was just an asshole.

Shaking her head, she carried on opening letters.

"You seem a little upset." He sipped his brandy and stared at her.

"It's called working. One of us has to do it. You don't have anything to do?" Her words came through gritted teeth.

"Not today, love. Perks of being in charge. Everyone else does the work for you. With proper guidance, of course. Remarkably, it gives you plenty of free time." He leaned back in his seat with a smug grin.

"Good for you. I do believe I understood your elaborate and much-appreciated guidance. So if you don't mind, I'd like to get on with things."

His face hardened as if his someone had just killed his dog. Had nobody ever told him to stop hovering before? No wonder his house staff looked so damn ragged all the time. Did he never think that maybe his employees would like to just do their work?

"I suppose I'll let you get on it then." He showed her a devilish grin. "Get on with it, I mean." He snatched the bottle of brandy out of the room and shut the door behind him with a soft click.

She stared at the door for a short while. His obvious innuendo at the end, what did that mean? He was hitting on her. She was sure of it, but at the same time she wasn't sure. He had to just be fucking with her for fun. It'd been too easy to get him to leave. But it was easy the first time, and he'd returned to bother her all but five minutes later. She wasn't going to get too optimistic.

As the day rolled on, though, she didn't see him again. Usually, she would be pleased her client was gone. But somehow, she wasn't. It annoyed her.

Anytime footsteps passed in the hallway, her head would snap up, and butterflies would swarm into her stomach. She'd curse them, get pissed at her body for betraying her.

He'd practically stalked from the room the last time, like a teenager who'd been told to stop doing stupid shit. And, much like that sort of teenager, she suspected he was going to try and find a loophole to do as he pleased, regardless of any of her suggestions. Maybe he was mad at her. Good, if it allowed her to do her job more effectively.

As the sun slowly set and she carefully put the papers to one side, ready to continue organizing them the next day, there was a soft, polite knock at the office door. It creaked open and the butler peered through the crack.

"Mr. Spencer wishes to see you before you leave, Miss."

Christina nodded. "Now is good. I'm done."

"No, he asked me to bring you to him."

"Okay." She nodded once more and looked over the table. It should be fine. She was at a good stopping point and would be able to carry on where she left off. Walking up to the door, she smiled at the butler. He stared, turned around, and walked down the hallway.

Christina followed through the house. It felt like being walked through a modern art gallery. The ceiling was tall, the marble floors gleamed, the clicking of her heels echoed across the huge empty spaces.

"In here, Miss." He made a sweeping gesture. It felt like being transported back to Victorian times. Surrounded by polite, tired, sour-faced servants who did anything their master asked of them. Who even had a butler these days? And how did someone manage to replicate the structure of a Victorian house without keeping any of the order and efficiency? The world Matty Spencer lived in was a strange combination of modern and old.

The room she walked into, on the other hand, was very modern. Maybe a little bit too perfect for her tastes. It was like a bedroom taken directly from a designer's magazine. The four-poster bed was made of twisted steel and covered in delicate floral patterns. The red velvet bedding matched the immaculate curtains, already drawn over the windows. It was barely lit by a faint orange glow from an array of industrial-style lamps.

She turned her head and tried to tamp down her anger. Her entire body heated at once.

Matty Spencer lay right in the middle of it. He was on top of the covers rather than under them. He was completely undressed and lounging there in nothing but boxer briefs.

Christina wasn't sure what to do. Her usual response would be to tell him to fuck off and walk right out of the room, however, she thought maybe that was the reaction he was after, judging by the grin plastered across his face. For some reason, Mr. Spencer's primary occupation seemed to be one of making her uncomfortable.

"I just need a report so that I can rest easy. Know I'm in good hands." Matty grinned.

Christina stared off at the wall and tapped a foot on the ground. "I've organized about a third of what needs to be done in the office. It will take a week before I can create a schedule for your household." Her words came out fast and on each short breath of hers.

Don't fucking look at him.

"Just don't get distracted." His grin widened farther. "By all the paperwork, that is. Nor forget that I have other things which need addressing."

Christina bit the inside of her cheek and did her best not to throw something at him, or glance over at the sleek contours of his finely-toned body. "Shouldn't be a problem. I'm not easily distracted." Her words came through her gritted teeth.

"Come here." He patted the bed.

Christina thought her heart might leap through her chest. Her breathing became labored, palms slickened, and it took everything in her power to compose herself.

She hated that he affected her this way. Why couldn't he cease being ridiculous for all of five minutes, and let her do her job and leave?

He picked up his cell phone. "So I can show you my schedule."

She should just tell him to email it to her. That was what she always did. Why was she walking over to *his* bed to look at *his* damn phone? Her body was betraying her brain.

She needed to show some self-control, some professionalism. Her face needed a slap, or a bucket of ice water thrown on it. She made her way over and sat down on the edge of the bed, taking the phone from his hand and glancing at it. She couldn't help but notice that the butler had left and shut the door behind him.

Matty's hand rested against her stockinged thigh as she scrolled through his weekly schedule. Excitement built in the pit of her stomach. The tips of his fingers were like fire on her leg. Electricity coursed through her, and her mind went to complete shit. It took everything she had to will herself to focus on the screen.

She should stand up, give his phone back, and walk out.

Without thinking, she uncrossed her legs and felt his hand glide up her inner thigh. Her breath hitched.

It only took a moment, but his hands slid to her waist and pulled her back against his hard chest. His skin was warm and smelled of body wash.

As his hands slipped around her, she knew she should've slapped him—told him off like she always did when clients got handsy. How could he be so forward? Confident? Act like she was nothing more than his property, to do with as he pleased?

But she didn't stop him. She couldn't.

The tension between them all afternoon had been palpable. He locked eyes with her as she was nearly seated in his lap.

His hand slid up her thigh again, finally resting on the top of her stocking. He grazed her exposed flesh at the line where the elastic ended with his fingertips.

His hand dug firmly into her thigh. "What do you say then?"

CHAPTER FIVE

Adrenaline coursed through Matty's body. This was it. She hadn't known it when she walked in that morning, but she was going to be his. That was often the way it went. Few women walked into his house with the express intention of ending up in his bed. Most had not even considered it. Most of them wanted it, but believed he was out of their league. That was usually true. But if he wanted them, they ended up on their back. That was the way of Matty Spencer's world.

And why not? He was a highly desirable man. He knew this. And if he desired a woman, and she desired him back, then it was only right for them to enjoy each other for a few hours.

He most definitely wanted Christina. And, from her response so far, she seemed to want him just as much.

The soft, smooth flesh of her upper thigh drove him wild. He wanted to rip those stockings off and feel her silky legs crossed behind his back as he fucked her mercilessly. Even though she was so stern, so serious, everything about her screamed sex and sensuality. In his experience, he'd learned that the most uptight of women usually were the wildest in his bed. Christina was the entire package—gorgeous and clearly repressed sexually.

Even now, as he embraced her with his hand roaming up her thigh, she remained calm and collected. But he could feel the heat from her pussy. Beneath her coldness she was still a woman with needs, practically begging for him to take it.

He pressed his lips lightly to her neck, and exhaled warm breath down her skin, just to watch the tiny hairs rise to attention. He sucked down her neck, hard enough to leave a mark—a reminder that she had surrendered her body to him. He wanted to mark her— let her know that all her coldness, professionalism, and defiance meant nothing to him. She was his.

His cock had already risen to the challenge, ready to make sure she was thoroughly broken and satisfied—a sweaty, chaotic mess in his sheets.

"Let's get you out of this dress, shall we?" He ran his tongue along the shell of her ear, reaching for the zip that ran down the length of her back.

It was as though his words had woken her up from a trance. She startled. Goosebumps pebbled on the back of her neck, and she tensed all at once.

"I'm busy." Her words came out on a gasp, and she shoved him back as she rose from the bed.

"Busy?" He gawked at her, perplexed. "Thought the work day was over?"

He leaned back a little in the bed, enough to give her a view of the massive erection tenting his boxer briefs. Matty wanted to provide her with a perfect view of what she was passing up.

She smiled politely, but he saw her eyes glance at his dick. Her tongue poked through her front teeth, and then quickly retreated. "It is. I need to get going."

"Need to get going where?" He could already feel her slipping away, and he found himself wanting her to stay, even if it wasn't to have her brains fucked out.

"Somewhere that's not—" She paused and looked around. "Here." Her heels clicked on the floor as she marched to the door. She stopped before opening it and he felt a sudden surge of adrenaline rush through his veins. Perhaps she was rethinking things?

She set his mobile down on the little dresser to her right, then turned to the door and opened it.

"See you tomorrow," he said.

"We'll see." She walked out of the room.

Matty's stare moved from the hall to the empty crease in the bed where she'd just been sitting, then over to his phone. Yep. She was gone.

What in the actual fuck?

Had he missed something? She'd been completely receptive to his advances. She'd moved to sit on his bed, next to him, as he lay there practically naked. She'd spread her legs to allow him access to her pussy, which he now regretted not taking. Matty smiled as he thought about the mark he'd left on her neck. At least that gave him a hint of satisfaction.

And sure, it was a woman's prerogative to change

her mind. But this sudden turn had completely baffled him. He'd thought it was a done deal once the legs opened up.

He was used to a little resistance. Or to someone asking to meet him the next day, or at the weekend. Or to the usual, "I have a boyfriend, please don't." And he knew just what to do or say in these situations. Remind them the door was right there, ask them to leave, and watch as they turned around and said that it was okay, that they would stay a bit longer, but he had to behave himself.

And in most cases, this resistance was just an excuse to make themselves feel better about the debauchery in which they were about to engage. Maybe they didn't want to seem too slutty. Maybe they didn't want to be caught cheating. Or maybe they just didn't want their boss to know they were banging his client.

All of them always had one thing in common, though. They desperately wanted Matty's dick inside them. They were just unsure of the social consequences.

It merely took a little finesse to show them that he could be trusted to keep it private. That he didn't care about their image or who they might upset. After that, they would relax a bit. And after a little of the ol' push and pull, they would eventually wind up beneath him, screaming his name.

He always made good on his side of the bargain too. None of his conquests had been broadcast, nor had they been exposed. And all of them had their wildest fantasies fulfilled. Just a quick romp and a polite goodbye as they staggered from his room. Because

Matty Spencer knew how to fuck, and he knew how to fuck well.

He was also used to some women not being interested at all. That was fine. He knew he wasn't everyone's cup of tea and, in fact, he'd half expected Christina to ask him to send her an email and walk right out of the room. That would've made a lot of sense too. A very small number of women were genuinely in a relationship with someone they were loyal to, or they were a lesbian. It happened on occasion. But this little experiment had told him that Christina wasn't so noble as to resist his charm. It was good to know she lacked at least a tiny bit of self-control. She'd shown her hand before she left.

Not that it would bother him if he didn't claim her eventually. What was the odd failed conquest or two? The vast majority of women all but begged to get into his bed before the day came to an end. He always made sure they didn't regret it. They might meet up again once or twice after that, but then he'd avoid them like the plague. Some women seemed to think the opportunity to fuck Matty meant a relationship. That was always an unfortunate and unsettling conversation.

But his theory of the nice, clean divide between girlfriends, lays, and uninterested women had always been supported by the data. They either wanted him or they didn't.

But not Christina. She had things to do. Things which were, apparently, more important than the night of her life with one of the world's most important men.

Perhaps he ought to give her a little more space. She

would, no doubt, come back to him. Whatever had
scared her away wouldn't last. She just needed a little
persuading.

———

Rising early the next morning, he decided to make a
good impression on her. She didn't like that he was
unorganized and boyish? Fine. He could be sharp and
professional if that was what it took. He would prove her
wrong, simply to rub it in her face. Let her know she'd
made a mistake.

He stared in the mirror and adjusted his tie, simultaneously feeling like an absolute idiot. Some of his friends
insisted that a suit that was expensive and original
enough could look relaxed and youthful. He didn't agree
in the slightest.

He only wore suits because they conveyed power,
and it helped draw the line between employer and
employee. Suits command without asking, and the last
thing Matty Spencer wanted to waste time with was
ordering people around to do shit that should be easily
done on its own. There was also the fact Christina wore
impeccably-pressed office wear, even though she was not
working in an office, so he would make sure that he
dressed twice as well as her.

Walking into his office, he was surprised to see that
Mr. Johannes had already let Christina in and she was
hard at work filing papers. By the looks of it, she'd been
there for an hour at least. He paused just outside the

door and stared at her for a few seconds that seemed an eternity. She looked amazing yet again.

She wore a fitted burgundy suit dress like it was a second skin, hugging every curve, seamlessly merging with her bronzed shoulders and neck. Her hair was tied firmly back and shimmering in the sunlight that streamed in through the window. Her makeup was as sharp as if painted on canvas by an artist.

"Good morning." She furrowed her brow. Christina had definitely noticed the suit, but he couldn't tell if she liked it, or if she was prepared to remark on it.

She looked back down at the papers and carried on with her task.

"You're early."

"Here at a normal working time, Mr. Spencer. There's a lot of work to do. Not all of us can sleep in and get away with it."

His hands balled into fists at his sides, but he wouldn't give her the satisfaction of getting to him. He nodded and watched her hands swiftly gliding over the table. Usually, he wasn't even awake this early, much less dressed, and much, much less working. It was too overwhelming, first thing in the morning. He needed a coffee and some time to relax before he could even be bothered to open an email. And then he would need his breaks during the day.

But not this woman. She would just sit there and work. How did she do it? His own attention span lasted him an hour at most. Judging by the pile of papers she'd managed to sort, she'd been going strong the entire morning, fully focused.

Incredible.

"Too bad you left so early last night. I hope you made it where you needed to go."

She shook her head and kept her eyes glued to the papers. "To be fair, I didn't have anything I needed to do. I was simply uncomfortable."

Bitch.

"You didn't seem uncomfortable when you spread your legs on my bed."

Christina coughed as if choking and then quickly composed herself.

Matty couldn't help but feel like he'd got one up on her. He rather enjoyed getting a rise out of Christina.

"I was when you asked me to take my dress off. I shouldn't have been on your bed at all. Our relationship needs to remain strictly professional."

The hell it will.

Matty grinned wider, loving how uneasy Christina appeared. "Why?"

"Because I'm here to do a job, not to find a date."

"Who said anything about dating?"

Not that Matty wouldn't mind a date with Christina, but he had a reputation to maintain. A date, huh? Now there was an idea. But she would no doubt shoot it down instantly. She seemed to be determined to backpedal from what she had done last night.

"You're making my point for me, Mr. Spencer."

Well, he wasn't about to say it was wrong to hit on her. She'd embraced him. She'd encouraged him. And as soon as she walked away, he'd stopped. He'd done nothing wrong at all. If it was wrong for a man like him to make advances on a woman like her, especially when she practically invited him to, then he didn't want to be right, ever.

She'd have to be a lot more determined than this if she wanted to put him off. Especially now that she'd confessed her interest in him. How did she expect him to back down now that he knew he stood a chance? Women were so perplexing at times. Always denying themselves pleasure for the sake of their image.

"How about a business meeting over a meal?"

Christina looked up at him and raised an eyebrow. "Subtle." She returned to her paperwork.

"I'm serious. Would you like to discuss the plans you have for this house over a meal?"

"And what does that look like?" She set her papers down again.

"Perhaps you'd like to go to dinner with me tonight? We'll go out somewhere nice, have a bite to eat and a glass of wine, then talk about what you've seen and how you plan to rescue me from the disaster that is my life."

"That sounds a lot like a date. Which I specifically said I didn't want—" she made a show of looking at a non-existent watch, "around thirty seconds ago."

"I simply want to discuss things over a meal."

"Why don't we do it right now?" She stared with her sharp brown eyes.

"Why not later? I'm a busy man. I have many things to do today."

She nodded at him. "You appear very busy."

"Look, it's just a thank you dinner. For all the hard work you're doing. I know some amazing places."

"I've been to dinner in London before." She continued to swipe through papers.

"Sure, but I know some places you could never afford, and I'd like to treat you to one. Anything on the menu that you want." Matty's lips curled up into a grin. Surely that'd do the trick.

"I'll think about it." Her words came through a flexed jaw.

How could she be like this? He was giving her an opportunity to go out for dinner at one of London's best restaurants. Where she could better get to know a man she obviously wanted to fuck. Part of his brain told him he was working far too hard trying to impress this woman and win her over.

And what was he getting in return? She was playing hard to get. Like some sort of a teenager. This was the woman who accused *him* of being immature? A woman who could not acknowledge her own desires and reconcile them with her work and life?

Well, it wasn't going to work. He refused to lose. One way or another, he would get her.

CHAPTER SIX

What was it with this guy? Apparently, the word 'no' didn't mean anything to him. The more she thought about it, the more she realized this was the way most men behaved, so it really shouldn't have surprised her. Most men would insist on pushing her buttons, pushing her limits, trying to get her to do things she had explicitly said she wouldn't do. Usually, they gave up after she shut them down firmly.

But she hadn't shut Matty down firmly. In fact, she'd given him every possible opportunity to push her limits.

She needed to make it clear to him that she was not interested at all.

Christina looked up as the door swung open and Matty Spencer made his way in for the fifth time that morning. Perfect.

"Guess where I've been?"

"Out of the office? Not bothering me while I work?"

"Oh good. The attitude is back, I see. Is it some sort

of a defense mechanism, like when a cat puffs up to make itself look big?"

She glared, but couldn't help admitting to herself he was right. That didn't mean she'd tell him though.

"I don't have time for this. If you're not going to let me work, I'll quit."

He shook his head. "I'll only be here for a few more seconds, then I'll leave you alone to continue your intimate bonding with my backlogged post. I know how much you do enjoy envelopes."

She sighed heavily and ignored his last sentence. "Hurry up, so I can get back to work. I still have a lot to do."

"I just booked us a table at *The Grill* in the West End. Newly opened, actually staffed by celebrity chefs."

Christina paused, ran the sentence by herself again and, still not making sense of it, made direct eye contact with Matty. "Why?"

"For our business dinner tonight." He smirked as if she should've caught on the first time, which she had.

"Dining alone might be bad for your image."

"Don't worry. You can bring my mail with you, work at the table. Multitask as they say."

Heat rushed into Christina's face. "What makes you think I don't have plans already?" She hadn't shut him down yet, she thought. Why hadn't she just told him no? Why did she goad him? She knew the reason and it frustrated her even more.

"We both know that's not the case."

"It seems like an inefficient way to conduct business." Still hadn't shut him down. *Do not agree to dinner with him, Christina.*

He stalked toward her and her pulse sped up on her neck. "We both know this is going to happen. Everyone has business dinners." He paused. "And it's a perfectly efficient way to conduct business. Are you suggesting you can only sort the mail under these lights?" He smirked and stared at the lamps in the room.

She began to speak and he cut her off.

"There is something to the lights, isn't there? I'm sure it's the optimum condition under which one could pay bills."

"This is exactly the reason why I'm here." Christina shook her head, but caught herself fidgeting with a pen on the desk. "Just because other people are having business dinners doesn't make it a good idea."

He scrubbed a hand through his hair, clearly irritated with her stubbornness. "It's a meal at a nice restaurant where I can drink wine and talk about business surrounded by beautiful things, rather than cramped up in a stuffy little office. It sounds like a very good idea to me. I'd prefer it to this room."

She stared at him in desperation. He was only a few feet away and she thought she might suffocate. "Do you ever think about anything other than what you want?"

His mouth curled up into a smile. "Absolutely not."

Christina's jaw tightened. "Do you ever ask yourself if you should do it? If you can afford to do it? If it makes sense to do it? We don't just do things because we want to. Humans are not animals."

"Actually, they are. You just think you're better than

an animal." He shrugged. "Please forgive me for offering to buy you dinner." And with that, he turned around and slammed the door on his way out.

What a child.

He left her alone for the better part of the afternoon. She wasn't sure whether she was happy or irritated. It was good in a sense. This meant that she'd have plenty of time to get ahead on her work. But it was also irritating. He'd walked out on such a bad note, in such an awful mood. Contrary to popular belief, she didn't enjoy people being upset with her. She did want to tell him what she thought of his toddler-like behavior, though. He needed to accept it when someone told him no. It wouldn't achieve anything, of course. It would probably just anger him more. But she had a lot of thoughts and feelings that she was bottling up right now.

Normally, social interactions came naturally to her, the way she could read people and adjust. A little frustration was easy to lock away until she went home, and then she could get back to her flat and either spend a night watching movies with the cat, or get changed and go work out. Something to burn off the steam. But it was hard to hold back everything she felt when she was around Matty. Something about him was different, and it ate at her constantly.

The door swung open and he walked in holding a sheet of paper. He seemed just as angry as he'd been when he walked out. Possibly a little more. But, he marched right up to her and dropped it on the table.

She picked it up. It was a hand-drawn chart covered in numbers and columns. Some were astronomically high. Some were only a few hundred pounds. It would probably make more sense if she went through it on her own, but she didn't have that kind of time on her hands.

"What is this?" She looked over the page at Matty.

"Proof that I can afford a bloody meal at a restaurant."

She scanned the sheet again. With context, it made more sense. It wasn't the best job, definitely not created by an accountant. He'd probably just dug up this week's profit and loss statements from his bank account, as well as the restaurant's menu, and then pieced it together himself. Him taking the time to do it made her want to smile. Clearly, he wanted to have a meal with her.

"Did you go out of your way to put this together?"

He nodded. "I did. Seeing as *apparently*, I need to provide scientific evidence to enjoy my dinner. Happy?"

She hadn't expected this. A man of his stature jumping through hoops just for her. Doing something he'd clearly never done before, just because he thought it would impress her. "Yes." She muttered the word under her breath.

"Come again? Couldn't hear you."

She scowled, but it was a fake scowl with a smile threatening to break out from beneath it. "I said yes."

"So, is the dinner permitted now?"

She sighed heavily. "Is it really important to you?"

"Isn't that apparent? You saw the trouble I went through. I didn't peg you for one to ask inefficient questions."

She held back a laugh. He really was playing this game? She should turn him down right then. It would be fun to take down a guy with an ego like his. Even a simple rejection was enough to anger him.

But she didn't want to turn him down. If she were honest with herself, she knew she was intrigued by him. She really did want to go to dinner with him and find out what he wanted to do and say, how he thought he would win her over. What could it hurt, anyway? A good meal with something nice to look at. It would definitely be more exciting than watching movies with the cat.

"Okay." She handed the paper back. "The evidence speaks for itself, Mr. Spencer."

A smug grin spread across his face. "See you there at seven, then." He snatched the paper from her hand and left the room.

She picked up the next envelope, ready to get back to work. But her focus was shattered. Had she really just done that? Had she agreed to go to his dumb business dinner with him? A dinner that would no doubt be private. An excuse to sit next to her and hit on her.

She'd only been on one business dinner like this before. She'd been naïve and assumed the client was being professional. She'd only made that mistake once. But this wasn't a mistake. This was an actual opportunity, which she was practically handing to Matty on a silver platter. That was the problem. She was almost certain her body would betray her brain again if she went through with this. She'd have to will herself to stay away from his bedroom.

Arriving at the restaurant, she looked around, wondering how exactly this whole dating thing worked. The setting was definitely not professional. Had she really expected it to be? Of course not. That was why she'd slipped into her little black dress and done her hair up a little more relaxed than usual. She knew what kind of a dinner this was going to be. She was there on her own terms now.

As soon as she mentioned her name the server bowed, took her coat, and showed her to one of the private booths right next to the kitchen. She could see the two celebrity chefs personally cooking their dinner. And in the booth sat Matty, already sipping a glass of wine.

He raised the glass to her. "Good you could make it."

She sat down at the other side of the table as the server poured her a glass of the same wine. This wasn't too bad. It wasn't professional, but it wasn't sleazy or romantic either.

"You didn't bring your work with you. One would think you actually came to enjoy yourself." His shit-eating grin brought heat to her face.

"Oh, I'm capable of enjoying myself, Mr. Spencer. In the presence of certain company." She matched him with a smirk of her own.

The booth was nice, and the low lights glowed on Matty's face, bringing out his high cheekbones and sharp jawline. The leather of the seats was soft and luxurious. The aroma of steak filled the whole place and caused her stomach to grumble. Matty started talking to her about the restaurant, its origins, the ideas the chefs had, the design. He'd completely ignored her retort. She couldn't tell if it was on purpose, or if he'd just learned to brush her insults aside.

Conspicuously absent from the conversation was the job she'd been hired to do, the problems with his life, and the plans she had to help him. Not that she minded. Before the food came he'd regaled her with the entire history of the restaurant, and they'd finished half the bottle of wine.

Perhaps she should at least give him a chance? He wasn't that bad. His mind seemed to hold onto so many random facts, information about trivial things. He was a genius when it came to talking about food, music, and cars. It was too bad that he couldn't apply his intellect to his actual business.

He went to pour her another glass. She realized she'd already had a couple of hundred pounds worth of alcohol. He could more than afford it, as she'd seen on his makeshift spreadsheet. That still confused her, too. But she still felt bad about drinking wine that expensive. It wasn't like he was going to get what he wanted. She put her hand over the glass.

"No?" He lowered the bottle.

She shook her head. "I'm good for now."

He raised an eyebrow. "Pacing yourself?"

"I don't want to get drunk. It'd be bad news around you." Her words didn't come out as sharp and professional as she usually liked. They were much softer, kinder. She knew she was warming up to him. But she shouldn't. She had to keep this exactly as it had been planned—professional.

"I understand that." He lifted his hand to attract the server's attention. "Could you get her something non-alcoholic to drink?"

The server scurried off to get the drink, and she turned back to him. "Figured you'd prefer me drunk?"

"I wouldn't want to take advantage of you. You'll come to me of your own free will."

She scoffed. "Is that what this is? Some show of chivalry to get me to lower my guard?"

"A way of getting to know one another. And so far, I like what I see." He stood and moved around to take a seat beside her.

As it always did whenever he came nearby, her heart kicked up about three notches above normal. "And I guess you're going to wait until I finally fall for you?" She moved her stare to the kitchen to watch the chefs flambé something. The flames licked toward the ceiling in a brief, angry flash.

"Precisely." He took another sip of his wine.

His close proximity sent goosebumps pebbling up her arm and neck.

"You'll be waiting a while. I don't sleep with clients."

"What about men you go to dinner with? Do you sleep with them?"

"Sometimes, but not with my clients." She suppressed a smile and noticed Matty's hand clutching a fork so hard the whites of his knuckles showed.

"I think we both know it's only a matter of time." Matty winked at her.

A fucking wink? Is he kidding me right now?

She couldn't believe how arrogant he could be some-times. The thought of messing with him seemed like a fun idea. He needed to be brought down a peg or two.

"Like I said, Mr. Spencer." She winked back at him. An obvious fake wink. "I don't sleep with clients."

"You also said you don't go to dinner with your clients. And yet, here we are."

Before she knew what'd happened, he'd leaned in next to her ear. Her heart pounded in her chest, and her palms became slick.

"Maybe I'm not a client after all."

She turned to face him, her brown eyes meeting his sharp blues. She wanted to reply, but she couldn't. Her throat had completely closed off, and any sound she tried to make would certainly catch. He really was one of the most handsome men she'd ever seen in her entire life. Even looking at him was difficult. She lost control any time she made eye contact with him. And, after all, he was right. What harm would it do?

Matty lingered for a moment. He stared into her eyes like he was looking straight past her cold gaze and staring deep inside her. He leaned in, straight toward her mouth. Her vision turned to explosions of fuzzy dots, and her entire body tingled with anticipation.

She leaned in.

His lips met hers.

The explosions turned into fireworks. Electric currents zipped through her limbs and bloomed across her skin. He tasted fantastic. She ran her fingers through his hair, pulling him even closer so that he couldn't

SHAGGED 65

break the kiss. His hands found her hips and yanked her into him, forceful and strong. His mouth moved along her neck, the same place he'd left a mark that she'd had to cover with makeup that morning. He made her crazy. So insane that she'd forgotten to scold him for it earlier in the day.

The kiss was incredible. But it was wrong. She pushed back, breaking his hold on her waist. She immediately wanted to jump right back into his lap, but she knew it would only lead to disaster. Both of them panted for air. His face was flushed, and his eyes were still hungry and half-hooded. She wanted to kiss him again. She wanted to do much more than that too. But she just couldn't, regardless if she was floating on air at the moment. That would fade, and Matty was still, well, Matty.

"I can't," she whispered. "I want this to remain professional. Please respect my wishes."

"You kissed me as much as I kissed you."

She shook her head. "It was a mistake."

His fingers grazed her cheek and pressed a few stray locks of hair behind her ear. "And what a fantastic mistake it was."

"We have to keep this professional."

"Why do the two need to be mutually exclusive?"

She hesitated. She wasn't really sure. She'd made it a rule years ago when she'd first started. But that was more to get rid of the men she wasn't interested in. She'd always been aware of how attractive men found her, and she'd wanted to avoid the issue. Saying she had a rule against sleeping with clients was easier than convincing some self-absorbed old man that she found him repulsive. But she actually liked Matty. So why was she applying her rule to him?

"It would be a distraction. I should be focusing on my work and getting the job done as efficiently as possible. Romance and sex would get in the way of that. It'd prevent me from doing my job."

"I understand. Except for one fucking thing—" He slowly inched toward her face.

"Which is?"

"You're still here."

She was. She was still there. For all she was saying, she was still sitting right next to him, thigh-to-thigh. She tried to convince herself that she was doing her very best to be detached and professional, yet, she stared at her lipstick smeared across his mouth, and his hair disheveled from her hands.

She leaned in and kissed him again. This time she gripped his hair twice as hard as before. She couldn't help herself. He was raw sex and power and blue eyes that seared to her bones. And even if he was a complete idiot when it came to managing his life, he had so much more hidden behind his eyes. She couldn't go on telling herself he was nothing but an immature idiot. He was different than her. He had a few more layers to his identity than the average guy. And that difference, that mystery—it thrilled her.

CHAPTER SEVEN

"Finally." He sighed as she leaned in, gently licking his lip. He opened his mouth to her, intent on taking what he wanted. He licked back, battling for dominance. Usually, he won this fight easily, as women rarely pushed back against him. But Christina was nothing if not a challenge to the core, and she joined in on the battle, exploring his mouth with confidence.

At the end of the day, Matty knew it was all an act. She could pretend to be dominant all she liked—believe she was in charge. The fact of the matter was that he'd won, and it was a sweet victory. She'd tried to resist his charms, tried to deny her own desires, and had failed spectacularly at both.

He'd finally cracked her shell and been rewarded handsomely, with more prizes to follow. There really was a woman under all that. However cold, however mechanical, however orderly and straightforward she tried to be, at her core she was pure female. Sensual, passionate, tender, gleeful, giving, afraid. She'd done her very best to hide this from the world and from herself. But it was still under there, waiting for the right circumstances to break free.

She finally gave in, letting him into her mouth. His hands tightened at her waist and then slid up to her shoulders and neck. Then he reached down with a free hand and ran it up her thigh. She gasped with surprise and pleasure, and his lips smashed harder against her mouth.

She tasted divine. Sweet and mild, with a hint of berries from her lip balm and a hint of sugar from her soda cocktail. He knew that her perfectionism would extend to everything. No doubt her entire body, from head to toe, would smell and taste of berries, just like her lips did. He was eager to find out just how wonderfully delicious her pussy was, and he planned to find out what his name sounded like on her lips when she came undone with her legs wrapped around his head.

Breaking the kiss, he glanced at the table. The waiter had brought them their second round of drinks, but must've noticed their intimate moment and held off bringing appetizers.

"Why'd you stop?" Christina frowned.

"We'll catch dinner tomorrow." He pulled out his wallet and tossed a pile of notes on the table.

"What? Why?"

He raked his gaze up and down her body. "I have another menu in mind."

She gave him a sternly disapproving look.

Not this shit again. "What is it now? You can't leave a meal that's already been started?"

"You're a slow learner, aren't you?"

He paused, running through the situation in his mind. He'd ceased kissing her to pay his bill and go home to fuck. He'd put the money on the table. He paused. "The money?" He made eye contact with her. "You want me to pay the exact bill?"

"And leave a tip for the server."

"Perhaps whatever doesn't go toward the bill *is* the tip for the server?"

"Okay, how much are you tipping them?"

He sighed. "I thought we were leaving work behind for tonight?"

"I thought this was a business dinner, and you wanted to change your lifestyle and habits for good, not just during office hours." Christina folded her arms over her chest. It pushed her breasts together right in front of Matty's face. He found it hard to pull his gaze away from them.

There it was again. The coldness and attitude he was more familiar with. He'd started to wonder if the old Christina was still in there.

"Fine, I'll pay by card." He put the notes back in his wallet, save a bill for the waiter. Damn, she was difficult.

But she did smile when he'd asked for the card reader and paid the precise amount he owed. In fact, she seemed almost satisfied. The way he felt when he managed to find the time to make a painting, or when he sealed a new deal. She probably looked just as he'd looked when she first kissed him. Seeing the world in order really was that important to her.

He'd met people who enjoyed order and balance before. But she seemed a far more extreme, convoluted version than he'd ever seen. In his experience, even a person who adored order would make some exception for the chaos that naturally surrounded him. But Christina did not. When he was acting as she expected him to, she was happy and loving. And when he was acting in a matter she didn't care for, she reverted to robotic formality.

She was something else, she really was. She was such a tight ass, that disorder actively turned her off. Surely, once he'd fucked her properly, she'd loosen up. That had to be the issue.

After the bill was paid, they made their way swiftly back to his house, where he immediately led her upstairs.

Walking into the bedroom, she retained some of her confident defiance. He wasn't sure whether he loved it or hated it at this point. All he knew was that he wanted her naked in his bed, in the fewest steps possible. He loved the push and pull. But he wished she'd push a little less, and pull a little more, preferably on his cock.

He chuckled to himself and closed the door behind them. She remained erect, head high and proud. He wanted to sweep her off her feet and into the bed, to take her immediately. But he knew that wouldn't work. She wanted to dance the dance. She wanted him to seduce her.

Fortunately, for Matty Spencer, that came all too

easily for him.

He walked up and unfastened her hair clip before she could protest. The crisp, sharp edge of her tightly bound hair broke, and locks of wavy brown cascaded down onto her shoulders and over her chest. They bounced and shimmered in the amber light of his lamps. The sleek, mechanical finish had been stripped away to reveal a soft sea of hair.

He looked at her lips. The sharp lines of her lipstick were initially resistant, but he'd begun to wear them down, and a light smudge appeared around the edges. He wanted to smear it. He wanted to erase that sharp red line entirely—do away with the harshness that surrounded her body and reveal the curvy, wild animal beneath the armor.

"Absolutely beautiful." He made a slow circle around her and traced a line with his index finger over her collarbone, before slipping the dress from her shoulders. It caressed her curves as it fell, pooling at her feet in a pile of silky fabric. She flinched, as though it had hurt. As though by removing her makeup and dress he was actively cutting pieces off her body, bulldozing the walls of her very existence.

He continued kissing her, admiring the goosebumps rising all over her bronze, exposed skin. As each layer of her personality stripped away, she became more and more vulnerable under his hands, more and more receptive to his advances. It was all building up to the ultimate surrender, the culmination of their dance where he would possess her entirely.

Glancing down at her naked body for the first time,

he was pleased to see how warm and inviting her soft brown skin was, in contrast to her sharp, pitch-black dress.

It was structured, but with a feminine edge. A delicate pink, with a white lace overlay. Her suspenders were a dusky pink, fading down into her slightly reddish stockings, the colors graduating in steps, down to the sharp red under her heels.

Releasing her from his grasp, he moved to the bed, ripping off his own shirt before sitting down and sliding his trousers off, all while keeping his gaze locked on her. She had a perfect hourglass figure, with a vertigo-inducing dip from the flare of her hips into the curve of her waist. Her thick, luxurious hair framed her face, and her breasts were high and firm. Her legs were toned, yet soft, gently compressed by the top of her stockings. She was so helpless, yet tried to remain proud. Such an intense rush of adrenaline coursed through Matty that a groan caught in his throat. He noticed bows at the top of her garters. She was like a little present, all wrapped up, begging to be devoured.

She delicately stepped out of her dress and followed him, black heels with red soles clacking sharply on the floor. He could see why she wore them. They demanded respect and represented authority. All the things Matty enjoyed defying. Their extreme height elevated the petite woman to challenge most men's stature. Their sleek lines and told him they were expensive. She didn't need a man to support her. They screamed independence and control. And the rhythmic click said that she did not mind being seen, that her every movement was important, that she was worthy of attention and admiration. It was all an act. Matty knew she felt the same butterflies kicking in her stomach. How could she not?

It was in this moment he realized she truly was giving him a gift. She was showing her vulnerability. All that sweet, feminine tenderness was his to own and enjoy.

As she drew close enough to touch, he gripped her hips firmly, and dug his fingers into her soft, tender flesh. She let out a yelp of approval.

In one smooth motion, he turned and threw her down on the bed, forcing a gasp out of her. He climbed on top and slanted his mouth over hers. His growl landed on her lips. She tasted even better like this, helpless and naked. She bit his lip. Not angrily, or in rejection, but not softly and tenderly either.

If Matty knew one thing, it would be that Christina would not be running this show. He tasted copper on his tongue, and ran a hand down her thigh and yanked it up over his hip, giving him deeper access.

He pinned her wrists over her head and sucked down her neck.

"Holy shit." Christina gasped.

He tasted the salty-sweet of her neckline and traced his tongue over her collarbone, before working his way back up to her ear. "I run the show now. Understood?"

She nodded with an eagerness he'd never seen from her.

He sucked down on her earlobe and ended by clamping his teeth around it. "Good," he said through his teeth.

He reared up slightly, forcing her hands and teeth to let go, and watched her sink back into the silky red sheets. Her hair was loose and tangled, spreading out beneath her like a blanket. Her lipstick was smeared. He enjoyed her disheveled, out of order. It was how he planned to keep her. Her breasts threatened to escape from the top of her bra. She was breaking under him, and it sent a surge of epinephrine coursing through him. She wasn't a dominant robot woman anymore. He *would* tame this feisty woman and show her the night of her life.

With a quick, sweeping motion he grabbed both her wrists in one hand, and with his other, he palmed her breast and rolled her nipple between his thumb and forefinger. She smirked defiantly and began to twist her arms, trying to break free. It was a pointless effort. Even if she'd been trying in earnest, a woman her size stood no chance against a man who no doubt weighed twice what she did. Even so, he slid his hand from her breast to her throat. A little move Matty enjoyed immensely.

She froze on the spot, her smirk fading to a meek smile as his hand ever so softly caressed her neck, squeezing lightly, teasingly. At any moment, they both knew he could bear down and cut off her air supply.

"I'm going to taste you." He smothered her mouth with his, taking whatever he wanted with his tongue, before pulling away. "And then I'm going to fuck you."

He grinned at her and she shuddered with anticipation. She nodded lightly against his grip.

"Good girl."

CHAPTER EIGHT

Christina couldn't believe what she was doing. She'd never stood naked with the lights on in front of another man, let alone allowed one to grab her by the throat. But fuck, it felt so right. Shocks of tingles pooled between her thighs anytime Matty so much as breathed on her. She'd never been heated up in this way, experienced this type of excitement in the bedroom. She'd tried to wrestle back control from the very beginning, but it was a useless attempt. As long as she wanted him, she'd do anything to enjoy him. Anything he wanted.

And now, the full weight of him pinning her down, his large hand gripping her neck, she gave up the last bit of fight she had in her.

She sucked in a breath when his mouth met her breast, and he took her nipple between his teeth. Fireworks went off from the tips of her fingers down to her toes. Heat rushed between her legs, and tension in need of a deep release landed in her clit. She was nearly on the cusp of an orgasm and he'd barely moved at all.

It was something in the power Matty held over her. She was helpless, and had quickly learned that she definitely enjoyed the feeling, when she never thought she would.

He eyed her cautiously, as if her surrendering to him was some kind of trick. Maybe he thought she was just sitting there, waiting to strike when he was vulnerable. He leaned over, and his mouth hovered a short distance from her ear.

"Behave." His word was a growl, and sent another delicious shiver down her spine. Her brain threw up every warning flag on the planet with Matty Spencer. This was wrong. She shouldn't be doing this. She didn't need a man to boss her around and do whatever he pleased to her. But her body responded to every touch and sensation as though she might die if it were taken away.

In the end, her body won out, as she knew it probably would. She'd be anything he wanted her to be, as long as he didn't stop.

He sat up and released her wrists. As she moved them down he shot her a disapproving glance. At his fierce gaze, she smiled meekly and put her hands back above her head, and rested them on the pillows.

"Good girl." He paused there, admiring her body as if she were his next meal.

She stared back at him, taking in every line of his figure, every defined muscle shining in the orange lights, and every bead of sweat trickling down the contours of his hips and abs, down to the vee that pointed below his belt. When her eyes landed on the huge dick bulging against his boxer briefs, she instinctively looked away, just as she had last time she'd seen it. She quickly turned back and stared at his cock. It was so hard she could make out the head pressed against the fabric.

"See something you like, love?"

Christina nodded like a child that wanted to play with a toy. It looked long and thick—even through the fabric, she could tell it would be a challenge to fit inside her. She swallowed hard. It might even hurt.

But she wanted it. She wanted all of him. She gently raised her left thigh so that it grazed his stiff prick, solely for the purpose of feeling his erection against her skin.

Before she knew what'd happened, his knee was between her legs, and he spread her thighs with it, much harder than was needed to receive the result he was after. She gasped and spread them even wider for him.

His hand trailed down over her stomach and rested at the hem of her panties. She arched her back, which angled her pussy up toward his face as an offering, teasing him and at the same time allowing him to remove them.

"You're going to get yourself fucked proper if you keep this up."

Jesus, his filthy British mouth. Christina found that she loved it. Almost as though sensing her need, he pulled his own thigh back and leaned over her. She locked eyes with him and he smirked while simultaneously shaking his head. She frowned and arched her back again, still feeling his hand on the hem of her panties. He pulled them down and slid them from her legs, leaving her bare.

Then in one swift motion, his mouth surged back toward her face and he cupped her shaved pussy in his palm.

He bent down to her ear. "Mine."

"Shit." Her word was a jumbled gasp as his rough fingers massaged and squeezed her. His thumb swirled around her clit in slow circles, while his eyes remained locked on her face, seemingly taking in every bit of information about how she reacted.

"Oh, I do believe you rather enjoy that, don't you?" Two of his fingers sank deep inside her.

She squirmed and cooed, and her hips rolled with each thrust of his fingers, trying to take them deeper and harder.

"All that pent-up sexual frustration. I'd dare say you needed a good finger fucking, didn't you?"

Christina was already lost in the moment, so close to a release. It was as if she were on the edge of a cliff with someone holding her back, not allowing her to take the plunge. She realized it was Matty. His fingers now drilled in and out of her, and his thumb still stroked her clit. He was watching her. Anytime she got close, he would slow down and prevent her orgasm—the worst torture imaginable.

He made a tsk tsk sound as if he could read her thoughts. "Not until I say so."

Christina had never begged for anything in her life. If she wanted something, she made it happen. She worked her ass off for it. Begging was beneath her.

There was nothing in the world that she couldn't achieve on her own.

Matty seemed to tear down everything that made her who she was, because the next words out of her mouth surprised even her. "Please. God. Please."

For shame, Christina.

The corners of Matty's mouth curled up into a wry smile. His fingers sped up until her mind was utter shit, completely unable to concentrate.

"That's good, love. I like it when you beg."

Christina was so close her body actually ached, throbbed for release. Her hands shot out and gripped the bedsheets, crumpling them around her grasp.

The feelings were all so intense, she'd lost track of where Matty even was. That question was soon answered when she heard him say, "Come for me."

And then there were lips.

His mouth.

It suckled her clit while his fingers drove into her, the fingertips curled slightly upward to hit the ridges deep inside her.

Black and white spots danced in her vision, and a wave of electricity rolled through her limbs and blasted out of her fingers and toes. Euphoria ripped up her spine, and her back arched, nothing but her feet and shoulders made contact with the bed. Matty's mouth remained locked on her, and his tongue stroked her clit furiously. If she lowered her hips, his mouth went with her.

She convulsed, nearly seizing up, as the strongest

orgasm of her life completely destroyed her body in the best possible way.

A moment later it subsided, and she lay there, panting, staring up at the ceiling with wide eyes. His mouth slowly kissed up her stomach, all the way to her tits. She threw her head back and moaned when his tongue swirled around one of her nipples. She couldn't believe how hard she'd just come on Matty Spencer's mouth, lying on top of his four-poster bed.

Her nipples hardened under the gentle graze of lace as he unclasped her bra. Before she could begin to make sense of what was happening, he bit down on her nipple once more, his tongue flicking against the tip lightly. She moaned and brought her hands down to his head, pressing him into her.

All that went through her mind was how bad she wanted him inside her. Her body was already tensing for another orgasm, and if it was even half as good as the last, she'd be good for at least a month.

Matty looked up at her while he still palmed one of her breasts—licking, sucking, biting. Like a typical male —obsessed. She caught him smiling up at her with a devilish grin, and she found herself wondering what he had planned. She could only pray it ended with his cock shoved into her.

While she still pondered what Matty might feel like inside her, he gripped her once more, and in one swift motion flipped her over onto her stomach. Christina was not accustomed to being tossed around, but the sudden movement and the force at which he'd grabbed her—it lit another flame inside her that surged through her body and licked at her fingers and toes.

She began to resist, simply as a natural reaction.

Matty's hand smacked square onto her ass with a loud crack. The stinging pain ripped up her back and jolted her mind into another world. She'd never imagined being spanked in the bedroom. Most of the men she'd been with simply seized on top of her for a bit and then rolled over and went to sleep.

Matty was a different beast altogether, and clearly comfortable with his role in the bedroom. "*Ow.*" The word trailed from Christina's lips—but not as a cry of pain. There was a burning need behind it, a need that sent her mind into a frenzied state.

Matty's mouth was next to her ear again before she could get all her wits back. "I do believe that you just enjoyed that too, you dirty little slut."

Another bolt of lightning scorched through her at his filthy mouth. No man had ever talked to her in that manner, and yet, somehow her pussy ached for more, and a pool of nerves swirled down to her center like a funnel.

She still panted from the initial slap, when another crack rang out and that delicious stinging pain shot through her legs and up her spine once more.

"Yes."

Matty's hand slowly slid up her back, tracing the contours of her shoulder blades and beyond, and then she felt the one thing that could send only more pulsing need into her clit. His fingers raked into her long locks of hair and balled into a fist. His knuckles pressed against her scalp, and he pulled her ear closer to his mouth, while he exhaled warm breath along with his words. "I didn't catch that last part. So tell me, do you enjoy having your ass spanked by a powerful man, Christina?"

She nodded against his hold, her breathing labored, but no matter how much her brain told her she was being degraded, she couldn't resist. He owned her. He'd broken her. The pleading came from her mouth before she could filter it from her body.

"Yes, please. More. Yes." Breathing was a struggle. She'd never been so overwhelmed with passion in her life. Her pussy was on fire and she could feel her wetness coursing down her legs onto his thousand-count Egyptian sheets.

"That's *my* good girl."

She felt that cold, sinister smirk against her cheek, and she couldn't help but notice the emphasis on the word 'my.' So possessive, and yet cleverly laced through his words. No matter how much she wanted to fight it, she'd never been turned on like this, and she would worry about the accompanying shame later on. It was future Christina's problem, because holy shit, Matty fucking Spencer.

He pulled her up to him by the hair, and her back pressed against his rock-hard chest. He reached around and cupped one of her breasts, taking his time to make sure and keep every ounce of pleasure bottled up inside her body, and at the same time teasing her to a point she might pass out.

"You enjoy torturing me. Don't you?"

He massaged her breast some more. "Oh yes, love. You can guarantee that I do."

He pinched her nipple so hard she nearly cried out, but sucked in a huge breath instead, unwilling to give him the satisfaction.

"I love when you beg for me. There's nothing in this world that makes my cock harder, you see? Or perhaps you should feel for yourself."

She reached back for his cock, and he snatched her by the wrist and pinned it behind her back. "You forgot to ask for permission to touch my cock."

There was nothing she wanted more than to feel his length in her palm. Her brain was a haze of nothing but pure, unadulterated lust.

"May I touch your cock?"

His hand tightened in her hair and he growled into her ear. "May I touch your cock, *Sir*?"

Her breath hitched once more at his forcefulness. "M-may I touch your cock—" She hesitated. Old Christina—the staunch conservative, feminist in her—reared her ugly head, trying to persuade her to not lose all her dignity. It was a fruitless effort.

She could practically feel a grin spreading across Matty's face as she readied to say the word. Christina swallowed hard, as knuckles dug into her scalp, and his other hand squeezed her wrist even harder. "*Sir*."

Her eyes flicked to her side and noticed Matty had leaned around to stare at her face while she said it. She scowled at him, but they both knew it was nothing but a show. The back and forth made the situation that much more intense. It was part of what made it all so exciting.

He smirked and led her hand by the wrist.

Her hungry fingers grasped back, her hand searching for what he'd promised her. She found the head of his cock first, by far the largest she'd ever felt. Her fingers wrapped around the crown, squeezing his wide girth in her palm. She thought for a moment about tightening her hold on it so hard that he passed out from blood loss. That'd be a nice lesson to teach him for spanking her like a child and making her beg, but she couldn't.

Her wet pussy still throbbed with need, and if she denied him, she thought she might die. Her hand slid down his length, for what seemed like forever, until she reached the base.

Jesus, can that fit inside me?

Her hand stroked back and forth over his huge cock, her eyes growing wider each time. She could easily wrap both hands around it with room to spare, and she found herself licking her lips, hoping she'd feel it in her mouth before the night ended.

It was a crazy thought. She truly felt she might be losing her mind right then. Never in her life, had she wanted to suck a man's cock, though she'd done it a few times. It definitely wasn't something she ever sought out to do. What was this man doing to her?

"What do you think we should do with that situation?" Matty nodded down at his dick in her hand.

Christina was too infatuated with searing every feeling onto the hard drive in her brain to even hear what he'd said. She wanted to capture every sensation and log it away, in case she needed it for a solo session down the road when Matty was unavailable to service her.

She found herself at a loss for words and hadn't had time to brace by the time she realized Matty had let go of her wrist. *Crack!*

Her hand stroked him even faster at the swift pain that shot through her ass and legs, and this time a moan escaped her lips instead of a whimper. He was using operant conditioning on her. She knew this. She'd studied psychology in school. He was programming her brain to want the sweet, delicious pain, and she was helpless against him.

"Fuck," she moaned on an exhale.

"I asked a question."

"Please, Matty. Please fuck me."

"Oh yes. That's what I like to hear." His hand slid down between her ass and cupped her pussy from beneath while she continued to stroke him. "I'll tell you what I think." Two fingers slid inside her, and her pussy clenched around them at the sensation.

"Wh-what's that—" She paused. "Sir?" The word came much easier this time, and she already knew that it'd made him happy by the tone of his voice.

"My God, you're so fucking tight and wet." His fingers slid in and out, slowly at the moment, as if he were savoring each stroke. "Exquisite."

She nodded at his words.

Without notice, he thrust his fingers to the hilt, as far and as deep as they'd go. She moaned at the sudden intrusion and the pressure with which he forced his fingers into her. "I think I'll stretch this tight little cunt. Necessary, you see, if it's to take this cock."

"Oh my God." Her words came on a heavy exhale and ended with her taking in a sharp breath.

"Any. Which. Way. I. Fucking. *Want.*"

He smacked her hand away from his dick. His fingers splayed across her back and he shoved her face-first into the bed. Her hands braced her on each side, and she instinctively went to push herself back up. However, another sharp crack rang out through the room, and his hand slid up to her neck, to the back of her head, and forced her face into a pillow.

"I said behave, love."

This is it. He's finally going to fuck me.

No matter how hard her brain tried to resist, her back naturally arched and shoved her ass into the air.

"Yeah, that's it. Offer that pussy up like the dirty little bitch that you are."

Holy. Fucking. Shit.

Christina braced for his cock, but instead felt Matty spreading her cheeks apart, and warm breath playing across her ass and pussy, as if he was examining her.

"This pussy, love. Just fucking perfect." A flick of his tongue across her clit followed his sentence, and then he licked all the way up to the puckered ridge of her asshole.

She squirmed and tried to pull away. No man had ever gone anywhere near that area, but his hands gripped her curvy hips and pulled it next to his mouth. His warm breath tickled her sensitive skin.

"If I didn't know any better, I'd think you wanted me to lick your ass, Christina."

"You're so fucking dirty."

He spread her cheeks even farther, opening her up to him. "Oh yes. You'll need a shower when I'm done with you."

She felt him adjust behind her on the bed, and once more, braced for his cock. Instead, he smacked the head of his huge prick forcefully up into her clit. Her thighs clenched, and his fingers on one hand dug into her waist, hard enough to leave bruises. She could only assume he had his cock fisted with the other. She wanted to see it, but her view was blocked from the angle. He teased the crown all around the edges of her entrance in a slow circle.

Her ass tried to buck up against his hold, her pussy needy for any extra friction it could get.

"Bite down on that pillow. Gentle is not in my vocabulary."

Christina obeyed, almost without fully processing what he'd said. She was a slave to his words. She'd do whatever he asked until she got her release. It was too much. Too intense.

Matty pressed up against her pussy and parted her slick folds with the head of his cock. "So much for professionalism." He shoved into her.

Whatever words Christina had been holding in came out of her mouth, coupled with a series of moans and heavy panting, alternating between some Deity and Matty's name.

She'd thought it would hurt more than it did, but he definitely stretched her, and he was definitely not gentle.

"Fuck, your cunt's so tight. Just heavenly."

She jolted forward with each slick collision of his hips and her ass. Matty gripped her at the waist and seemingly yanked her into him as he thrust from the opposite direction. The man was a fucking machine. And it wasn't all over the place either. He fucked her with methodical, rhythmic surges, each angled perfectly to hit the magic spot deep inside her. It sent her mind reeling with pleasure.

She wondered if she would ever be able to fuck another man after Matty.

One of his hands slid up her back and into her hair. She quickly learned there wasn't much that was better than Matty pulling her hair while he pounded into her. If there was anything better in the universe, she didn't know what it was at that moment. Add in a swat to her ass and she was about to go over the edge of the cliff once more.

"Fucking hell, Christina."

She angled her head to get a view of him from behind. That was the moment she knew it was more than just him wanting to dominate her in the bedroom. Sure, it was degrading, and out of character in every other way of her life, but it was perfect at that moment, and by the look on Matty's strained face, he was definitely happy about it too.

The words and actions didn't matter, so long as they were both enjoying themselves and consensual. It was pure fun, and pure lust, and she wouldn't apologize to her brain for it later. Christina was letting her hair down, for once in her life—and allowing Matty to pull it.

She knew she was only a moment away from erupting with another orgasm, and from the looks of Matty, he had to be close too. Although he was in the position of power, Christina felt powerful too. She could stop at any moment and send Matty into a state of hysteria. That, in itself, was a form of control that she enjoyed, even as his giant cock slammed into her from behind, and he had her head wrenched up by her hair. If she told him to stop, she knew he would.

But, there was no way in fucking hell she'd tell him to stop now. Impossible, even if she wanted to.

Matty let out short grunts with each of his thrusts, which seemed to speed up with each second. Smacking sounds of wet flesh on flesh echoed through his giant bedroom. All four posts on the bed shook and rattled.

"Play with your cunt and come on my cock."

Jesus Christ.

Tingling sensations swirled to her clit, like water circling a drain, and she was about to lose herself. Her hand slid up between her legs, and she circled her clit. She'd never done anything like that for another guy. Hadn't ever come close to it.

"Permission to come, Sir?" She barely got the words out without fainting.

Matty hesitated for a moment, most likely in shock that she'd asked for permission in the heat of the moment.

"Yes. Come on my fucking dick. And say my goddamn name when you do it."

She closed her eyes, and fuzzy dots exploded everywhere. Her entire body stiffened, and her toes curled up against the sheets.

"Fuck, Matty. Fuck." His name fell from her lips over and over as the waves of ecstasy coursed through her limbs. The orgasm finally rolled through her body and subsided, and she slowly realized Matty was still fucking her, probably on the verge of exploding.

"Jesus, fuck. I'm so close." His words were strained, and his entire body was nothing but corded muscle and rough sinew. A fine sheen of sweat coated his chest and gleamed in the light.

Christina wasn't sure what came over her, but she reached back and gripped his balls in her hand.

"Fucking Christ, wom—"

She felt him ram into her as far as he possibly could, and his balls tightened against her hand. His cock kicked deep within her, and hot spurts of come went off like jets as he filled her to the brim. She massaged his balls, and clenched her pussy at the same time, over and over, as if milking him for every last drop.

She tried to push the thought that Matty had just come inside her far from her mind, and just enjoy the moment a little longer. Christina knew that she was about to experience a hangover of regret, for days, weeks, and possibly months, but she'd never done anything like this before in her life. She was entitled to one poor decision, and Matty Spencer was the best worst choice she'd ever made.

She released her grip on him and he sank back on his heels behind her, panting, and grinning like a complete idiot. For just a second, he looked like a schoolboy who'd just lost his virginity. She liked the smile she put on his face, knowing she'd made him feel as good as he'd made her feel.

"Holy shit, love."

His tall powerful frame glistened with sweat, and the light created a fine sheen that glistened over every cut of muscle. He looked like a statue that should've been in a museum somewhere, on display for public consumption, though she greedily loved that she had him all to herself right then.

Her mind was still a dense fog from the mind-blowing orgasm she'd just had, and she collapsed right onto her stomach. She shuddered lightly when she felt a bead of his hot come slide down her inner thigh.

He leaned up and kissed her cheek, as if he'd just morphed from a sex god into a perfect gentleman. The rough edge to him was gone, and he was relaxed and attentive.

"Stay right there. I'm going to get a towel and something for you to drink."

When he returned, Christina was passed out on the bed, snoring.

He shook his head at her. "Jesus, just like a fucking man. Got her rocks off and went straight to sleep."

CHAPTER NINE

The orange light began to project the artificial sun from Matty's phone onto the wall, and the sound of chirping birds filled the room. Matty slowly pried open his eyes and stared up at the ceiling. The streaks of blue began to appear as the fake sun rose above him, and he heard his coffee maker start up at the far side of the room, just out of view behind a screen and a slightly neglected house plant.

Matty was in a position he'd grown accustomed to over the years, but looking at Christina, this time it was different. The satisfaction he was used to. A new conquest, a great fuck, and a good night's sleep was always a beautiful way to start a day. But seeing *her* in his bed was a million times better, because of the initial reluctance on her part. And because of some deep feeling he couldn't put his finger on.

Normally that satisfaction felt complete, like after finishing a painting, or getting a new car. That joy of completing a task, and the slight disappointment that the journey had come to an end. It was supposed to be a final feeling, the full stop at the bottom of the last page of the experience. But it wasn't.

Rather, he felt the same way one did after a big meal. He enjoyed last night very much, but his appetite for her quickly returned. Just because he'd had a lovely dinner didn't mean he didn't want breakfast as well. He wondered if he'd ever have enough of this woman. The way she'd submitted to him, completely trusted him—it was like a narcotic in his veins.

The way she looked in his bed after they'd finished, when he'd returned to take care of her—he felt as though it could be more than just pure lust, and primal want. More than just a casual fling, or a conquest. Her face was almost angelic, and she'd fully given in to her desires. He'd found himself wanting to take care of her. Make sure she was okay. He'd had—actual feelings.

These thoughts didn't sit well with Matty after the initial elation of waking up with her next to him. Matty's life was tightly compartmentalized for a reason, and that included his love life, or lack thereof. Relationships were work, and Matty Spencer enjoyed the least amount of work possible. What was more, he was certain the moment she woke, she'd return to her cold, rigid personality. Probably worse, considering the regret she was sure to project onto him. It'd probably ruin his breakfast.

After a moment of contemplation, though, he was ready for more Christina. Their night together hadn't scratched the itch. It'd had stoked the flames even higher.

Usually, he'd already begun plans for the next girl by now. Or at least he no longer felt that intense craving. Even the women who wound up becoming his girl-friends for a while, didn't mean all that much after that first night. They were arm candy, or decent conversation, or the perfect plus-one for some event or another he'd been invited to. But as soon as he'd enjoyed them once, he knew he would be buried in another woman eventually.

Not so with Christina. Looking at her, he couldn't imagine himself fucking another woman the rest of his life. He didn't feel complete. He felt hollow. Even though she was lying asleep right next to him, he felt empty at the thought that she was not his, and he doubted she ever could be. Managing a woman like Christina would be impossible. She was an enigma, a unicorn. She marched to the beat of her own drum, and nobody could tame her. The thought of doing so would be absurd.

It was ridiculous. He'd taken her. He'd broken her. He'd owned her as much as any man could own a woman, surely more than any man had ever owned her. His hands tightened into fists at the thought of another man even trying. He'd marked her with his teeth and his fingers. That first moment he spanked her—he would never forget that. The thought of her begging him for more—Matty's cock hardened as the memory played through his mind. He'd watched her rough exterior crumble under his touch, and just for him. So why wasn't he completely satisfied?

He moved closer to her, and reached out under the covers, then wrapped his strong arm around her waist. He pulled her up against his body. She was so petite. Much smaller than she'd seemed when he first saw her. And so much softer. And so much warmer. Fuck. She was so feline, like a cat, lying there fully sated from the night before.

He wasn't even sure what he wanted from her, but as he watched her sleeping, all sorts of fantasies played out in his mind. Fantasies from marrying her, all the way up to tying her to a chair as she begged him to fuck her mouth—something he fully intended to do. But at the same time, he had thoughts of the sweetest, most meaningless romantic gestures he'd never even remotely considered before. Buying her flowers, strolling through a park holding hands. It was ludicrous, almost disgusting to him. But, he wanted to do it all with her. To give it all to her. To take it all from her. He shuddered at the thought that he wanted her as a companion. A lover. A friend.

He pressed his lips to her forehead tenderly, inhaling the sweet cherry scent in her hair, noting that it was infused with a faint note of his cologne.

She stirred, and then her eyes slowly opened to meet the day. Her long eyelashes fluttered against her soft skin. She was lovely. She looked at him so sweetly, so warmly—it was hard to believe she was the same person he'd hired two days ago. She smiled at him.

"Morning." She stretched her feline arms above her head and yawned.

He ran a hand through her hair, tucking a few stray locks behind her ear. "Good morning. Did you sleep all right?"

She nodded softly.

"I know it isn't always fun sleeping in a strange bed." He kissed her forehead again.

"The bed is perfect." Her eyes darted around the room and then widened. "Are those fake birds? And a fake sunrise?" She raised an eyebrow.

"That's Mia."

"The house computer?" Christina rolled over and looked at the projected sun on the ceiling.

He nodded and pulled her closer to him so that her head was nuzzled in the crook of his neck. With his index finger, he traced the soft curves of her gorgeous, naked body as if he were painting her on a canvas. The curve of her shoulder, along the swell of her breast, and down the side of her hip.

She rested her head on his chest. "Is she the one making coffee too, or is that one of the human servants?"

"That's the house," he said. "She does everything."

"How long 'til she replaces all the staff?"

"There's only one staff you should be concerned with at the moment." He was sure to press his still-hard cock up against her ass.

Christina rolled her eyes, but Matty noticed something he wasn't sure he'd witnessed. A laugh. He'd made the ice queen laugh. He was off to a good start for

the day. A better day already than he'd had in a very
long time—since he could remember, in fact. Something
about that struck him too. He knew he'd completely
satisfied her in bed the previous night, but the knowledge he'd made her laugh—the feeling was nearly as
intense as conquering her in the bedroom.

"I'm serious. Will she eventually replace your
employees?"

He sighed. "Well, she can't even do her own job.
That's why you're here. So I guess it will be at least
another decade or two."

It was nice to be able to wake up and talk to someone. Usually, there was nobody he wanted to talk to.
He'd much rather wake up on his own with a cup of
coffee. Even when he was with any of his past girlfriends he would ask them to shut up as he put on the
radio and went to get breakfast. If Christina was any
other woman, he'd have already left the room after
instructing her to get dressed and go away. Not so
much in those words, but he was a master of giving
hints.

But no. He wanted her to stay there, under his arm,
with her head on his chest, asking questions about the
future of his work—if that was what she wished to
discuss. He wanted to remain like this all day if possible
—cancel all his meetings, and just sit and watch
Christina, and listen to everything she had to say.

In his thirty-one years of life, he'd never experienced
anything quite like this. What was happening to him?
He barely even knew this woman.

He could lose his company, his money, his art, even

his cars, and as long as he was able to wake up like this every morning, it would be worth it.

If he was younger, he would've called this ridiculous notion love. But in his lifetime, he'd learned that love was nothing more than simple infatuation. It always passed. It would pass with her too, which was why he wouldn't mold any long-term decisions around the way he currently felt. He would not give up his company, his money, his art, or his cars just to wake up next to her every morning. Because she was sure to tire of him, or he of her, once all these new chemicals ceased to race through their bodies.

He'd learned the hard way about love.

And sure enough, the more Christina became aware of her surroundings, the less comfortable she seemed. Her face was slowly turning back to ice. She was most certainly replaying last night in her mind and applying those decisions to the future. Analyzing her entire life, the way she did with his stack of bills.

"I suppose you'll want to have a shower and get ready for work? Mr. Johannes can source you a dress. And at least you haven't got far to travel."

She obviously faked the smile that now appeared on her face. "A shower sounds great, actually."

He showed her to the en-suite, turned the shower on for her, and went to get his coffee. Sipping it and looking out the window at the London skyline, he wondered how he should play his current predicament. He sort of missed the cold Christina with the bad attitude, but he had no doubt he'd encounter her once more shortly. People didn't change who they were, especially strong-willed females like her. But he didn't mind this. It was no fun trying to break someone who posed no resistance. Perhaps this could be their little dance they did every day. She could be her usual self during the day, and at night, he'd just fuck it right out of her. He didn't want one version or the other—he wanted them both.

"Mia, call Mr. Johannes."

Mia lit up and dialed the number.

He sipped his coffee and, as the call connected, went to the wardrobe looking for a towel for Christina.

Mr. Johannes' face interrupted and ruined the beautiful projection of clouds on the wall. "Yes, Mr. Spencer?"

"I need a woman's suit dress in a size—" He paused and picked Christina's up from the floor. "It needs to be in a size eight-ish, I think. It doesn't have a label."

"I would assume that, with her figure, she would get them tailored."

"Yes." He dropped the dress to the floor. "Just find me one in every size from six to twelve and bring them in. And have a tailor on standby who can be ready to alter one at a moment's notice if she requires it."

"Of course, Mr. Spencer."

The phone call ended.

Matty glared at the projection of clouds as it resumed. Why was Mia so useless? All he wanted to do was continue his father's legacy as being at the forefront of new developments. And he'd seized something which was going to revolutionize modern life. He'd hired all the best minds in IT he could get. So why was Mia such a sack of shit? At the same time, he couldn't help but notice the irony. Were it not for Mia fucking up his life, Christina would've never come into it.

"You're not off the hook." He glared at the projection once more, as if he were talking to an actual person.

Hearing the shower stop, he wandered over to the bathroom, opened the door, and walked in. "Thought you may need this." He held out the towel.

"Thank you."

He handed it to her and she hastily covered herself up as though he hadn't seen and tasted every inch of her skin already.

"Need some help getting ready?" His eyebrows rose.

"I'm fine."

His jaw tightened at her declining the offer to assist her in getting dressed, which they both knew would actually mean undressing her. It'd half been a joke, but now he found himself wanting to strip her naked so that he could do whatever he pleased. Matty Spencer rarely asked questions. He gave orders. And despite the sudden walls she was putting up, he noticed the goosebumps pebbling over her naked flesh. Her perfectly shaved pussy flashed in his mind, wet with need. His cock rose, and he bit back a groan. He knew the goosebumps on her neck weren't from the cold air, but from his voice and presence. He rather enjoyed affecting her so much.

He didn't like the tone of her voice, like she was appeasing him, but wanted him away from her as soon as possible. Matty was a lot of things, but he knew he wasn't a repellant for women, and definitely not for

Christina. She'd begged for his cock the night before for fuck's sake.

"Do you mind? I should get back to work. I have to finish the office today." She seemed desperate to get out of his room.

"Mr. Johannes is bringing a selection of suit dresses for you. You can do your hair and makeup here as well."

She nodded. "Thanks."

He watched her move to the bed and sit down, digging through her bag for that little parcel of emergency makeup every woman seemed to carry. She began marking the lines with a slightly nervous, shaky hand.

Mr Johannes arrived soon after with the dresses and she found one that more or less fit her.

"Does it need tailored?"

Christina gave him a look. "No. We don't have time for that, even if it did."

Matty took a sip of his coffee. "We have one nearby ready to make any alterations you need, if it comes to that."

"You what?" Christina seemed perplexed.

"I had one called. In case you needed his services."

Christina's mouth curled upward slightly, and then quickly pressed back into a thin line. "That's okay, this will work." She stared at him for a quick moment. "Thanks, though." She turned away sharply, seemingly looking for a way out of the room.

She was so quiet all of a sudden, almost withdrawn. Once dressed, she took off for the door. Matty watched her walk away, heels clacking on the floor. The sight of her ass and hips swaying back and forth sent his cock warring with his zipper once more. Mr. Johannes followed her and Matty let out a groan and adjusted himself.

He made his way to the office, where he saw her sorting papers again, only this time with a little less deliberation than yesterday.

"You all right? You seem a little off."

She rolled her eyes, though she did it where she thought he wouldn't notice. "I'm fine. Just tired."

"I'm not surprised, considering everything. But it seems to be something more than that. You're not at all yourself."

She scoffed. "You barely know me. I'm very much myself."

He paused and stared at her. He had his doubts.

She sighed. "It's nothing. I just need to focus on my work."

She wouldn't fool him. Something was wrong. What on earth had come over her? She hadn't insulted him once this morning. It was as though having sex had ripped out some essential part of her being. Or perhaps she was just not able to wear that mask in front of him anymore. The harshness, the coldness, the detachment, had all been stripped away and she saw no reason to keep up the impression any longer? But why?

He'd known women who adorned different masks for every situation. Not as extreme as Christina's, but different nonetheless. But generally, they kept the two very much separated, and consistent. Christina did not seem capable of that.

She hadn't been a virgin, had she? She felt too experienced, and she'd have been in much more pain. And yet he felt he'd done something to her which nobody had done before, something which had fundamentally changed her. Perhaps nobody had broken her before. Nobody had managed to show her what she needed, and tamed her in the bedroom. If that was the case, then perhaps he had taken a virginity of sorts.

He ought to be happy with himself. But he couldn't help but feel bad. He'd unwittingly ruined one of the very things which had attracted him to her. The answer came to him. She'd fallen in love with him, and she didn't know how to deal with those feelings. That had to be it. Of course it was. He smiled to himself and walked from the room.

CHAPTER TEN

Christina wasn't sure what she felt about any of this. She knew she wasn't being her usual self, but she was also too distracted to be able to work *and* maintain her composure. She just wanted to focus on work, but it didn't look like it wasn't going to work that way. All she could think about was last night, and what a mistake it'd been. The regret had slammed into her the moment she woke up.

Matty frustrated her to no end. He was such an arrogant asshole. It was hot in the bedroom, but definitely not during the day. And then he'd do things like bring her a towel, and call up a tailor at a moment's notice, just in case her dress didn't fit perfectly. Who the hell did that? Like she would allow him to pay a fortune just to have her dress altered for a day. It was ridiculous, and wasteful. And at the same time, she couldn't help but swoon a little at how sweet it was. And he'd done it just for her. She cringed at her feelings.

Her whole life she'd always been moving towards goals, goals, goals. But last night had been unrestrained, completely exposed, mind-altering orgasmic sex. And she wasn't sure she liked it. Not the actual sex. Nothing had been better than that. But what had transformed inside her. She didn't know that side of her existed. She'd begged Matty for his cock for crying out loud. Her face flushed with pink hues at the thought. She wasn't even sure how she'd managed to do it. She'd never begged for anything in her life. Had she been completely drunk, she'd have said she was coerced. It was *that* out of character for her. But she was practically sober by the time they'd returned from dinner, and she definitely remembered doing it, agreeing to do it, and enjoying it.

She just couldn't understand why.

She liked Matty. She liked him a lot. But if this was who he was, then how could she commit to anything more than liking him? How could she end up in his bed, letting him dominate and own her, if he would never commit? And even if he wanted to, how would that work out? He'd be tired of her within a month, if not less. Men like him enjoyed a different woman for every occasion. She had no intention of ending up in some sort of lost baggage relationship where nobody wanted to come back for her. She wanted commitment out of a man, or nothing.

And it was too late. She'd already soiled a professional relationship. And now she wanted some kind of commitment from him. Commitment she would never get.

Her own commitment was a difficult question too.

She knew she needed to either reveal herself to him, in more ways than just physical, or she needed to keep up her professional attitude as though they hadn't fucked like wild animals. Neither of those options felt right.

Exposing herself, physically and emotionally, couldn't happen. He wasn't her boyfriend. She couldn't let a man that was practically a stranger inside. Couldn't allow him beyond the guarded walls she'd carefully built. But she already had, and had learned something new about herself.

How could she go back and pretend to be a stern, cold professional when he'd already seen her true self? She was a fraud, wearing a mask when he knew who she was.

She studied the stack of papers in front of her and damn near wanted to break down. But she couldn't. She had a job to do.

There was a reason that she'd drawn a line between the personal and the professional. A reason beyond wanting to turn down creeps and perverts. Because even when she actually liked a man, relationships ruined business deals. The whole situation was fucked up, complicated. She didn't know who to be and she'd lost all control. She wanted to go back to how she was before, but that was probably what had attracted him to her in the first place.

Christina had always taken pride in being mature beyond her years, a true professional. And now, for the first time since she was sixteen years old, she felt small, naïve, and like an idiot.

She convinced herself there was no way he'd take

her seriously after this. It was time to end their business relationship. It was the only way she could get her dignity back and recover from the shame.

She stood and stretched, then walked into the hallway. Her eyebrows rose in confusion at how empty it was. Usually, no matter what time of the day, servants always rushed around, cleaning or hurrying off somewhere. But now, when it would actually be convenient to see an employee, there was nobody there.

She gritted her teeth, determined.

Turning to one of the little screens on the wall, she wondered whether it was worth trying to get in contact with anyone. She could just walk out and pretend it never happened. But Christina knew she couldn't do that. Her mind wouldn't let her. She was a professional, and there was an adult way to handle this situation.

"Mia, call Mr. Spencer."

"Requesting clearance to talk to Mr. Spencer." Mia paused. *"Clearance not granted."*

"You've got to be fucking kidding me?" Mia was indeed useless. She inhaled a deep breath.

"Mia, call Mr. Johannes."

"Mr. Johannes is currently busy and is deflecting calls. Requesting password to override deflection?"

"Piece of shit." She glared at the wall. "Never mind."

"Playing 'Nevermind' by Leonard Cohen." Mia's voice faded to music.

Christina's face twisted and she clenched her palms. "Ugh." She felt like banging her head against a brick wall as the music increased in volume. She decided to walk up and down the giant house looking for Mr. Spencer, or a member of the staff.

She stepped out into the hallway.

"Mr. Spencer?" She peered down the empty hallway. Her voice echoed back at her. She walked toward the East of the house, where she knew that he'd spent a lot of his time the previous day. Maybe he would be there again.

As she walked along, Mia tracked her with motion detectors and played the song wherever she went. She whirled around in frustration. This was fucking ridiculous. How had he not ripped her damn cables out? Didn't it drive him insane? Or maybe it did. Maybe he was at his wit's end but dealt with it to keep up impressions.

As she walked along, she heard a different song come from a small hallway to her left. Something techno and high-pitched. It wasn't all that great, but it overrode Leonard Cohen, so that was something. The song faded, and as Christina stepped into the hallway, it abruptly stopped. The upbeat digital guitar continued. It had to be Mr. Spencer's own music.

Of course his music would be more important than everyone else's. But that told her he was nearby. The hallway had no doors to either side of it. It was just a narrow path leading to a single, plain white door. She stomped toward it and shoved it open with a forceful push. She froze at the sight, confused, wondering if she'd walked into another universe.

The room was insane. It was an amazing contrast from the rest of his house. It was ridiculously chaotic and dirty, and damn near caused her face to twitch. At the same time, it was gorgeous. There were large sheets, painted canvasses, and sculptures littered around. So many at the front of the room that she could barely see past them. What was more, they were filthy, coated with dust and speckled with paint. The marble floor had a single clear path, and then streaks of paint and piles of dust and reddish mud covered the rest of the place. It stretched almost to the edges, except for a few footprints that'd broken through the carpet of neglect.

It smelled like some sort of warehouse.

But it was also the most beautiful room in the entire building.

The tall ceiling looked like the roof of a greenhouse. It was at least fifteen feet tall, and the frosted glass was shaped into pyramid-like domes. It allowed natural light to penetrate every corner of the room. It felt brighter, bigger, and warmer than anywhere else in the house, since it wasn't Mia projecting some ridiculous fake sun.

Hundreds of paintings were strewn along the walls, all framed and carefully positioned. The display reached around eight feet high. Each one was a masterpiece. Like much of the rest of Mr. Spencer's house, the paintings depicted naked bodies and cars, but they were so much finer, and much more delicate. There was love and emotion infused into every piece. Christina had never had an eye for art, but she knew beauty when she saw it. The naked women were graceful and demure, the men modest and stern. The cars highlighted the engineering, structure, and power, rather than cost and status. It all formed a celebration of humanity, rather than sexuality or extravagance.

The sculptures that were uncovered were incredible too. The shapes were somewhat exaggerated, almost deformed, twisted to hide their joints and angles, yet still distinctly human. They were like soft dolls, intricately detailed to contain every human feature, but not quite real. And even so, their texture and shape were so stunning they almost seemed alive. She had to force herself not to pull the sheets off the others and have a look at them.

And the strange combination of chalky white and gray dust, red streaks of mud, and little drops of colorful paint made the floor look like abstract art. It was a disgusting mess, but somehow, she couldn't bring herself to hate it. It was an organic mess—but, looked like it belonged. She couldn't put a finger on it. It was almost like seeing sand in the desert or snow on a mountain. Dirty and unorganized, but exactly as it should be. It all just, worked.

Christina had never appreciated the arts. It wasn't how she was wired. But even someone as uncreative as herself could appreciate this in the middle of such a plain, sterile building.

She walked through and noticed something else— they were all unfinished works. Some of the paintings were completed, and some of the sculptures nearer the door were finished too. But most of what she saw was a work in progress.

One particular piece caught her eye. A giant canvas,

at least four by seven feet. It depicted a naked blue woman. She had the same softness, the same lack of human bone structure, as the sculptures. She was on a bed of emerald-green and ruby-red pillows, with her legs spread invitingly. But it wasn't just sexual. It was erotic. Everything was on display, but Christina could somehow see the humanity of her. It was as though by making the models less physically human, the artist had highlighted their emotional and mental features.

Someone hummed along to music and Christina spun around, startled. Half-hidden behind a covered sculpture, she noticed someone dancing to the music as he stirred a paint pot. It was Mr. Spencer.

He stood in front of a canvas and struck broad lines onto it in gray paint. The paint wasn't completely mixed, and every line was a unique blend of gray and white streaks. The only other colors on the work were red and blue, but Christina could already see the figure of a woman taking shape. There was an iridescent shimmer coming from the red on the canvas, picking up the light and bouncing it back onto his body. He was shirtless, wearing an apron to cover some very stained cargo shorts. He looked nothing like he had when they first met, nor how he'd looked the day before in his suit.

He was splattered with paint and glitter. His bare chest shined in the light. His arms were lined with various brush strokes, like he'd tested the paint on his own body. It looked like he'd just come from an explosion at an arts and crafts store. And he looked—fucking hot.

Just like the room itself, the chaos suited him. Sure,

it was dirty and all over the place. But it also seemed so natural, raw, and wild. It was like watching a caveman painting the walls, or like peering into a scene from the past, when humans were nomads. Not working behind desks, but bouncing from meal to meal, only stopping for a night of passionate sex or an afternoon of hunting. Her heart thumped against her chest.

Usually, she would run far away from a mess like this room, from stuff that could stain her expensive clothes or ruin her hair. But right now, she found herself wanting to jump all over him. She wanted that paint to rub off his body onto hers. To be covered in stripes and splatters—to be stained with his primal markings.

She started to back away. This wasn't right. She was there to turn him down, quit her job, and never see his ass again. She couldn't begin to try when the only thought on her mind was him pushing her up against the canvas, staining her back in blue, red, and gray.

Her heel hit a bucket of paint and it fell over. It made a huge noise, sending a stream of yellow paint next to her expensive shoes. She jumped and let out a squeal. Her breathing became labored and a shriek of fear shot straight up her spine. She backed away from the paint and rammed right into Mr. Spencer.

She gasped and turned around. He grabbed her before she could fall over. Her heels had been saved from the yellow river flowing from the bucket, but the black dress he had so kindly given to her that morning was now coated with paint that'd soared through the air.

"Sorry." She looked away. Tried to stare at anything

but his smooth, rock-hard muscles, and broad chest. "I ruined the dress."

"And spilled eight hundred pounds worth of specially mixed paint."

She shook her head. "I-I'm sorry. I shouldn't be—"

"Are you okay?"

She nodded. "Yeah. Sorry about the paint too." She glanced down at her heels once more, making sure they hadn't been ruined.

"It's no problem, I can get more. The wait is the worst part." He looked up at the canvas he'd been working on.

"You made these?" She stared back at the painting of the blue woman, and at the others in the room.

He nodded. "It's my hobby."

"They're incredible." She looked around the room once again, scanning every single item she could see from where they were.

"They're mostly unfinished."

"I noticed."

He smirked. "Of course you did."

"Why?"

He shrugged. "I get a new idea and want to try it out. Sometimes I just forget a project halfway through because it isn't working. Sometimes I leave it and pick up on it again when my head is clear. Can take me anywhere from a day to five years to finish a piece. If I ever finish it at all."

All the feelings and emotions in the room over-whelmed her at once. The man really was a damn genius. Not a genius in his field, but a fucking genius.

Why didn't he sell these? If only he could apply the same attention to his company, maybe he wouldn't be having so much trouble with everything—his house, his entire life.

He let go of her waist and picked up the paintbrush from the floor. Matty mumbled as he moved over to a little water fountain on a table, where he rinsed the brush carefully, removing traces of chipped paint and dust.

"Maybe if the place was neat and clean you wouldn't have that problem."

He shrugged. "Clay breaks into dust quickly. Paint dries and crumbles. I would be cleaning all day if I were to try and keep this place in order."

"You should have someone do it for you?"

He glared at her. "Fuck no."

She stared, blinking. "What?"

"Nobody is allowed to clean in here. Nobody ever has."

"I can see that. But it could use it. Then your brushes would stay clean, and there wouldn't be cans of paint everywhere for people to knock over. You'd be able to see across the room. A little organization would fix it right up."

He shrugged. "This isn't disorganized."

"It isn't organized either."

"I know where everything is. Everything makes sense. Things are always exactly where I put them, precisely as I left them. If someone else were to come in here and tidy I'd never know where to find anything, and it would never be within reach."

"That makes absolutely no sense to me."

He shrugged. "It doesn't have to. This isn't your painting room. This isn't your art. Nobody but me ever uses this space. So why does it matter if it makes sense to anyone but me?"

That was a good point. Christina spotted a chair and sat down. "Do you mind if I stay for a bit?"

"I'm not paying you to watch me work."

She nodded. Should she tell him? That was why she was there. To say she didn't want his money, or his job anymore. "It's my lunch break."

He flashed her a stern look. "Didn't know you knew how to take a break." He eyed her curiously, then nodded. "Okay. Just don't talk to me, touch anything, or clean."

"Not even the paint I spilled?"

"Especially that. It's a mark you were here. I like it there." He turned back to his canvas.

The familiar tingling shot through Christina's face and down to her legs. Jesus, this guy just said—things. Christina wasn't sure if he meant it or was joking, but she sat back and watched him continue to work as the yellow paint spread out slowly around the feet of the easels and stands. Something about what he said really resonated with her. The last thing she'd considered when she knocked over the paint was that it was art, or a reminder of her to him. Once again, he was sweet and kind, in the most annoying way possible.

She thought about things as she watched him slap paint around. Maybe she shouldn't end their contract just yet. She'd been afraid that she'd exposed too much of herself to him, but now, they seemed to be on a more level playing field. He'd shown her some of himself, even if it weren't by choice. Maybe she should wait and see what other surprises might be in store. She'd definitely liked what she'd seen in this room.

CHAPTER ELEVEN

Matty wasn't sure how or why she'd come to his studio. Normally, he hated anyone being in there. On one occasion he'd kicked Mr. Johannes out just for bringing his tea too far into the room. Everything was too frail, too personal, too private. Not to mention he'd gone there purposely to escape her. Give her time to work and for him to sort out these *feelings* he was experiencing. But no, she'd crashed right through another one of his walls, with no regard for his personal space.

He loved his art. Deeply and passionately. It was just something that made perfect sense to him when the world did not. No matter how hard he tried, he couldn't understand how most people could stick to deadlines, follow time without losing track of it, or do the same thing every hour of every day without going mad. It was part of the reason he'd created Mia, so he would have something to do all that dull work for him.

But even Mia made no sense at all. She got things wrong, communicated awkwardly, and created schedules that didn't suit him at all.

Only art made sense. And art was how he pushed the rest of the world away. Art could be messy and chaotic. It could be left and resumed with ease. Art was his little haven from reality. A person so used to order, so used to cleanliness and organization as Christina most certainly did not belong in there.

And yet, he liked having her there. He liked her watching him intently. Like all structured people without any artistic inclinations, she was in complete and utter awe of how his hands made the canvas come to life. Those people would never understand. They were the sort of person who painted by numbers and drew on a grid in art school. They could never experience what it was to feel art, any more than he could understand what it was to experience natural order.

But she seemed to appreciate it—see the beauty in all he did. And that was what counted.

She could stay. Just a little while, but she could stay. As he continued painting the woman's figure from his mind's eye, he realized that he was painting *her*. Stretched out, hands above her head, outlined in the reds, blues, and grays of her last three suits, her beautiful figure exposed, legs open, one side of the outline sharp and structured, the other half wild and flowing.

It was everything he saw in her, all her beauty. He felt fairly satisfied. But, it needed a nice deep brown too. Like her dark hair and eyes. Something to highlight her subtly warm soul, her strictness, her hidden passions.

He walked between a couple of sculptures, knowing exactly where he would find a warm mahogany paint, picking it up from the floor and swiftly marching back to the canvas.

"You can actually find your way around in this mess, can't you?"

"I know where everything is." He opened the small tin and dipped a fresh brush into it, wondering whether to leave it bold or stir some red glitter into it before painting her eyes and hair.

"How? There's shit everywhere. How do you find anything?"

"I suppose I just feel it." He snickered. "I know it sounds like bullshit, but I just know where something is going to be in here. In nature, nothing is alphabetized or put on shelves, and animals find their food and water just fine. I find my paints the same way."

"So, you're telling me you can *sense* where a can of paint is when it's halfway across this room, but you can't find a check on your desk?" She eyed him suspiciously.

"That's exactly what I just told you." He stirred some glitter into the brown paint, seeing the warmth and light bring it to life.

"You're a creative soul. What the hell are you doing as head of an IT company that's goal is to organize people's lives?"

"It's not like I chose it. I inherited the business from my father when he passed away. I suppose I want to do what he would have wanted from me."

"Why don't your two brothers take the business?"

He raised an eyebrow. "You really have done your

homework." Matty nodded lightly. "I do have two brothers. But surely from your detective work, you'd have
read that Ewan inherited another business that he'd
rather be working on, and Stephen spent all his inheri-
tance on cocaine. He just came out of prison two years
ago and is not to be trusted."

She looked away. "I-I didn't know that."

"It's not something we talk about much to the press."
He began to paint her hair in thick, curved strokes.

"But why not have Ewan take over? Or sell the business and focus on your art? Why keep working on new
computer projects that ultimately fail because you're not
passionate about it? It makes no sense."

"I like the money." He smirked at her.

"But you don't *need* the money." She looked around
at the room once more, seemingly in total awe of her
surroundings. "Nobody needs this much money."

"I didn't say *need*, I said *like*. I know I don't need it. I
just feel pleased when I see my bank account going up
every month."

She paused. "Wouldn't selling the company make
your bank account go up?"

"I already calculated that. I stand to make more if I
just keep working with the company. Long-term investment." He sighed in frustration. What was it to her if he
wanted to keep investing his time and energy into a
company he hated? She wasn't there to psychoanalyze
him, or fix his business. She was just there to make sure
he was organized enough to not miss meetings. He
stared at her over his shoulder.

"You're going to run out of money if you keep

making products that ruin people's lives like that fucking Mia." Her eyes met his.

"Mia was my father's pet project. He wanted to make a house that could look after itself, and all its inhabitants. I would at least like to see that project to its conclusion."

"Your dad ordered Mia?"

"No, my father designed Mia."

"Was your dad as bad at IT as you are?"

Matty whipped around, clearly annoyed at this point. "No, he was a genius. He just never completely finished her. We're having to iron out the kinks without him."

Christina nodded. "So, Mia was left unfinished? That makes sense, actually."

"Whatever did she do to you?" Matty's eyes went to the floor. He didn't enjoy hearing her rip apart his father's work.

"Well, I tried to call you and Mr. Johannes but she wouldn't let me, and then she played Leonard Cohen at me while I looked for you. I can't even remember the last time I heard Leonard Cohen before today. Probably at my grandpa's house. And it wouldn't go away until your music took over when I got to this room. That's how I figured out you were back here and found the place."

He laughed. "That's actually kind of funny."

"I'm sure it is when it's not happening to you." She couldn't keep her smile suppressed.

"She'll work out in the end. It always works out in the end."

"It doesn't for people who aren't loaded. Most people's mistakes cost them their business. Relationships, hobbies, even their lives."

"Mine don't. That's what matters."

"Until someone won't take your money, or it runs out."

He wanted to be angry at her. But she had a point. It only ever really worked out because he could afford to pay someone else to get the job done, or to lie for him. If the business truly went under, or they were sued for everything they owned, or someone wouldn't fix a problem for him, no matter how much he paid them, he'd be screwed.

He continued painting the thick waves of hair cascading down the gray woman's shoulders, the red glitter shining in the light the same way Christina's hair had shone when let loose.

He glanced over at her to admire her hair once more, wondering if she had worked out that he was painting her.

She was staring at her phone. Looking up, she made eye contact with him. She didn't seem as relaxed or as entertained as before. "I have to go. Another client's having trouble with his latest secretary and he needs me to help them out."

"Another client?" Matty's jaw flexed, and his fingers tightened on the paintbrush. "You have other clients?"

She nodded. "Uhh, yeah. This is a business, not a marriage. I try and give sixty or seventy percent of my attention to my newest client, to make sure they get the help they need, but I still go back to my old clients from time to time and make sure everything is in order."

"I thought you were only working for me today."

"I was. But Mr. Emery needs me more. I need to help him." She stood up and dropped her phone into her handbag.

"How are his needs more urgent than mine? You've seen what a mess everything is for me." He suddenly realized how desperate he sounded and straightened up. "Besides, you already began your work day for me. I'm not about to pay you to walk away, you know?"

"We'll pick this up tomorrow, but I need to hurry. I have to get changed before I get there. Can't show up in this."

He paused and looked at her dress, a bit confused. "It looks fine."

"It's covered in paint. I can't go to work covered in paint. *Look*, I will see you tomorrow. Thank you for understanding."

She walked off before he could say anything else, stepping over the still-creeping puddle of yellow paint. She disappeared into the maze of sculptures and canvasses. A few seconds later he heard the door open and shut. And he was alone in the studio again.

He stared at the painting before drawing a large brush stroke through the middle of the figure. Fuck that bitch. She'd completely ruined his inspiration. And he'd been on a roll too. It was looking so good and now he had no clue how to finish it. She'd just sat there getting paid to watch him paint, even if she said it was her lunch break. Bullshit. She'd eat something when she got to her house. He was sure of it.

He also wasn't sure why, but he'd thought they shared something special, something unique. He'd thought that her feelings for him were deep and meaningful. But apparently it was all just business. Apparently, last night hadn't impressed her, nor affected her, as much as he'd thought.

Wiping himself down roughly with a towel to remove some of the paint, he slipped out of his painting clothes and into a pair of plain jeans and a clean t-shirt. He couldn't do any more painting today. The whole artistic flow was nothing but muddled shit now. He may as well go to the office and see if he could do any work. If she was going to walk off like that, then he needed to know how to handle his own business. He didn't need her, or anyone else to tell him how to run his own damn life.

But he wanted her attention again. He hated her for that. Not actually hated, but she frustrated him to no end.

He sighed and decided to send her a bonus. It was how all problems were fixed, after all, wasn't it? Just send enough money through and she would have to come back. She herself had admitted to it. Everyone had a price.

Or had she meant that she was not going to be bought with money? Walking into the office and closing the door behind himself, he froze. What if that had been her subtle way of telling him that he had no power over her? She could not be bought. She would always have other clients, and she was not his own personal toy to play with.

And he damn sure wanted to own her. Now, more than ever.

He didn't want to marry. He never had. It hadn't worked for his father, or his brothers, or any of his friends. They'd all tried marriage, and all come out of it paying child support, losing a house, or just being bitter and miserable bastards with blue balls. He'd been put off that sort of contract for good reason.

But a long-term relationship was another matter. He'd dated a few beautiful women, almost monogamously, for a year or more. The experience hadn't exactly thrilled him. For all the fun of a long-term relationship with frequent sex, and for all the social merits of having a stunning woman on his arm, he always found the experience stressful. Most of these models and actresses and socialites were just in it to get a ring on their finger, swiftly followed by a divorce and a hefty payment. As soon as they found out that marriage was not an option, they'd magically vanish. And he'd grown so tired of the game that he hadn't dated seriously in a few years. It was easier that way.

Now, he felt tempted to give it another try. Not with a model, or someone whose main goal was to trick him into marriage for the sake of money. Just with a woman who was on the same page as he was. A woman who wanted a long, stable, happy romance without involving the government. Perhaps that was a good idea? Especially with a woman like Christina.

Someone who looked after herself. Who was smart

and calm. Who did not complain about things she didn't understand, like his art. A nice independent woman, who could get by on her own and not complain about him needing to take business trips, or be late at the office.

But if she didn't see their relationship as anything more than business, then what odds did it make? He had to see the arrangement for what it was. Just like she had not complained much about his art, he could not complain much about her work, her organization, her straightforward attitude.

He sat back at his desk and looked at the piles of paper she'd been sorting. He couldn't deny that she was doing an amazing job. And that was what he had paid her to do.

CHAPTER TWELVE

Christina sighed as she hung up the phone and started to type an email. At his age, Mr. Emery really should be handing the business to his daughter. She understood this world much better than he did. Unfortunately for him, part of his misunderstanding was that women were not capable of running a company.

Even though his daughter was far smarter, with a degree in business and another in accounting, her dad didn't trust her with anything. He wouldn't even let her answer phone calls for him, in case she "got ideas" about her place in the company.

He'd said she would only have a role to play in the company when she was married. Then her husband could take over the business and make sure she ran things correctly when Mr. Emery was no longer around to manage the place. If only he knew a little more about social media and the internet, perhaps he'd have known that Gracie Emery was a lesbian.

At least it meant Christina had work. Unlike other women, she was a trusted business partner for Mr. Emery. She was different in his eyes, though. She was calm and collected. She never wore her hair down or showed her knees under her dress. She didn't blush or giggle or even slap when she was hit on at work. She was bitter, snarky, and mechanical. As far as Mr. Emery was concerned, she wasn't a man, but she wasn't far off either. More like a robot, which he seemed to rank above women in terms of their ability to reason.

It was ridiculous thinking like this that got her most of her work. When she'd started out she'd wanted to just be herself. To be professional, of course, but also to be able to go for after-work drinks, joke around, and dress however she wanted. Make friends and just be normal. She'd learned fast because that was her strongest skill set. Adapting to her surroundings. Most of the people she made friends with in order to succeed at her job were like Mr. Emery—older men, from privileged back- grounds, with antiquated attitudes.

Smiling at them was flirting. Wearing something too bright or too low-cut was unprofessional. Going out for drinks was a date, even if there were ten other people there. There was nothing she could do that wouldn't be misinterpreted. There was no way she could carry herself that wouldn't ruin her career prospects. The best she could do was be cold, cruel, and hope they forgot about her quickly.

In fact, most of her employers no longer considered her a woman. The worst part was, she didn't really mind. They'd just give her work and let her focus.

Her entire childhood she'd been ashamed if she wasn't warm and friendly. But what had that got her? Condescension and oversight. The "bitch" always got the promotions. The "bitch" got respect. The "bitch" got a life. She was happy to star in the role of "The Bitch."

But now, with Mr. Spencer, that understanding had been turned on its head. He made her want to be a woman. Want to be vulnerable and sweet and kind. Not necessarily all the time, or at the expense of her identity and her work. Just sometimes. Whenever she damn well pleased.

She wanted to stop being a machine now and become human again. For him. She wanted to relax and just be herself. Not spend all day trying to avoid being judged. She wanted to be as natural and wild as he was. She wanted to let loose, and be a sweet girl or a bitch, maybe even a combination—to find her own identity as naturally as he'd found his paint in that chaotic room.

She knew he was against marriage. She knew that he was cold and detached from most people. She knew that he went through girlfriends like a teenage rugby player went through pizza at a buffet. There was no hope that he would change. Men like that never did. They just kept going—burning through girlfriends, having fun with whomever they wanted, and casting aside anyone who ruined their fun.

Christina could try and lie to herself that Matty Spencer was able to change. That *she* could change him, but it went against all her experience. He had an amazing life. He wouldn't just become a different person because she still held onto the hope of marriage, against all the odds.

But he was the most amazing man she'd ever met in her life. He was the most handsome, powerful, and natural person she'd ever been around. She never thought she could meet a client she liked, let alone fall in love with.

Especially him. When she'd researched him and his company, she was almost certain that she would hate him. He was the mind and the wallet behind Mia, the automated system that'd ruined so many of her clients' lives. He was the reason that perfectly decent people lost their businesses, or had to completely remodel their houses, all while he got richer.

But she was wrong. She couldn't even dislike him. He wasn't a broken monster. Seeing him in that studio was like watching a caveman. That was how people were meant to be. He wasn't some complete asshole, with his disorder, lack of punctuality, and poor filing systems.

She wanted nothing more than him. She wanted him to have her completely. And she wanted to surrender herself to him. She wanted to fall back to her primitive self and just *be*.

Everything else she did, from dressing that morning to sending Mr. Emery's final email, felt like a hollow attempt to extract meaning from a meaningless society. What was the point of any of it, if it didn't make her happy?

She nodded politely at Mr. Emery as she handed him two pieces of paper. An invoice and a report of everything she'd done. He seemed relieved and carefully read both sheets before signing the invoice at the bottom. He promised her a check in the mail as soon as he had a moment to write one out.

"Thank you so much." He stood from his chair.

"You're welcome."

It was odd. Normally it felt good to finish a job. Great, even. It was like her world was in balance, everything in its place—she'd created a little bit of order out of a clusterfuck.

But now she was like Sisyphus pushing his boulder up the mountain. What did it matter that she'd managed to keep Mr. Emery's website from collapsing? In a week or two it would fall apart again, and she'd be back in his office all over again.

It reminded her of what Mr. Spencer had said about the dust in his studio. That fine chalky powder which came from dry, smashed clay. It would creep, every single day, no matter what he did. It would take him most of the day, or a lot of money, to keep it from building up in the room.

Christina would've fought against it the entire time she was there. But Mr. Spencer didn't. He could produce one work a day, if he was inspired. And he'd lived in that house for fifteen years, according to her research. That was a theoretical five and a half thousand pieces he could've made. From what she'd seen there weren't nearly that many.

But it was still far more than she could've made. While she was spending her life fighting the natural disorder of the universe, Mr. Spencer had embraced it, and in doing so he'd created amazing beauty.

Christina left and drove home. Her flat was a world apart from the mansions and penthouses that her clients lived in. It was a small apartment with a tiny bathroom and a small kitchen area at the back. The medium-sized windows down one side of the room overlooked a quiet little alley.

It wasn't big, or grand, or full of expensive and interesting items. But it was clean, it was tidy, and it was home.

Picking up the mail, she realized she'd missed two days' worth. The morning before seeing Mr. Spencer, she'd left before it'd arrived. Since then, she'd only been home to change for dinner. She paused and sighed, looked around. It was early evening. She couldn't afford to wait much longer to go through the letters or she'd be no better than her clients.

The chaos constantly crept up on her. She could do whatever she liked to try and push back against it, but at the end of the day, it would always win. She opened a couple of bills and pinned them to her oversized calendar, specially made for her to organize everything. She threw a couple of fast food advertisements into the shredder, holding onto one for a kebab shop. A kebab would be nice for dinner after the day she'd had. Not healthy, or amazing. But tasty and cheap and there'd be no dishes to wash.

Her phone rang while she looked through the rest of the letters.

She recognized the number from America and knew

it could only be from one person—her father. He lived in Lexington, Kentucky. She leaned back against the wall. "Hello?"

"Miss Smith?"

"Yes."

"It's Doctor Stein."

Christina's heart dropped into her stomach. Her father had cancer, but it'd been in remission. "How may I help you?"

"I hate to say this, but your father asked me to call. He's not doing so well."

Christina blew out a sigh of relief, not at the fact her father was sick again, but she'd feared the worst. "I see. How's it looking?"

"Not good. I'm sorry."

"Tell him I'm on my way."

"Yes, Ma'am. There's one other thing while I have you."

"Yes?"

"I apologize, but there are problems with his insurance. We'll need to discuss that when you get here."

What in the hell? He shouldn't have any problems with insurance. She didn't have time to deal with that at the moment. She needed to be on the first flight out. "Okay. See you shortly."

Christina stood there in shock. It felt so surreal. The cancer had been in remission after an operation and radiation, and had shown no signs of spreading. He'd been well when he'd called her last weekend. Normal even.

Her heart was a hard lump in her throat. They'd been warned this could happen at any time, of course. She knew it could return. But, it wasn't supposed to happen to *her*, or *her* family. It was something that happened to other people.

She logged onto an airline website and booked the first ticket back to Lexington. Back home. She hadn't been home since Christmas two years ago. She moved to the UK years ago to study, and fell in love with the place, adopting their customs, and tastes. America was like a foreign land to the young expat.

She typed out an email to all her clients and booked herself a cab to Heathrow, then she threw her laptop, charger, and a change of clothes into a bag and walked out the door. All she wanted to do was cry, but she had to hold it together. She needed to be there for her dad. She could deal with herself later.

CHAPTER THIRTEEN

Scrolling through the texts and emails on his personal phone, Matty didn't feel as entertained as usual. The movie projected on the wall opposite his bed hardly thrilled him either, but normally a few angry texts would brighten his day considerably. A couple of days ago he would've found it hilarious to see his ex-girlfriends trying to get in contact with him, his brother complaining about his divorce, and his old employees begging for their jobs back.

After Christina, he just felt like an asshole. These were people who wanted him, needed him even, and he was treating them horribly. At least she had an excuse. She had a job. He wasn't all that important to her. These were people who had, at one time, mattered to him. And now he used their suffering for idle entertainment. To distract himself from the fact that his own life, however free of drama, was hollow and boring.

Then he saw it. An email notification from Miss Christina F. Smith.

Her name stood out like a neon sign, shining beautifully, and just inviting him to click on it. His heartbeat sped up at the thought that she was trying to get in contact with him. His mind was suddenly overwhelmed by a desire to read her words.

He fantasized briefly about what she'd say. Was she begging to get back in touch with him? Was she apologizing for how she'd behaved, leaving him for another client? Was she asking about his art? Another date? He grinned. Perhaps she wanted another night in his bed? Of course she did. Who wouldn't?

Most likely it was strictly professional. Arranging the schedule for the next day, or telling him off for being so disorganized. But a man could hope. Even so, he found himself incredibly eager to just see some words she'd put together for his attention.

He slumped against the pillow when he noticed it was a CC email, not one for him personally. He nearly deleted it without reading. But, it could still be important. Even if she was treating him like he was just some other guy, he should open it.

He lay back on the bed. "Mia, pause the film."

The film paused.

"Read email."

"To whom it may concern,

I'm sorry but I won't be available to work for the foreseeable future. I need to go home to the U.S. to deal with a family emergency. I've attached a list of colleagues who may be able to see to your imme-diate needs.

I apologize for any inconvenience this may cause, and will refund pre-paid appointments when I return.

Kindest regards,

Christina Francesca Smith."

For a moment the content of the email refused to sink in. The only thing he could think of was how she was, in fact, American, but not South American, as he'd assumed. She was North American, though probably not a descendant of immigrants.

He shrugged. She'd integrated well into the UK. Though he'd found something off about her accent. Her mannerisms were very British, and her knowledge of their customs and geography very precise. She'd been as meticulous about integrating as she was about every-thing else. It shouldn't have surprised him, but it did. Despite his business, he'd actually never been to Amer-ica. Only watched the movies and shows on television. She did kind of sound like them.

But that email—what a pile of bullshit. If she didn't want to work for him or see him any longer, she should've just told him. She wasn't normally such a pussy about things. She might've fooled the other idiots she sent it to, but he knew better. There was no family emergency. There was no trip back to America. She was just making an excuse. Perhaps because she was ashamed of what'd happened last night. Perhaps because she had too much work and couldn't keep up with the steady demand. Whatever the case, she was trying to inconspicuously get rid of some contacts.

It wasn't like he hadn't done this to other people before, of course, but this was different. He liked Christina. He'd showed her some respect—showed her his damn art for God's sake. Nobody else was privileged enough to see it. He'd thought that they shared something special, something different. At the very least, something that would require her to be honest about her intentions. Apparently, that was not the case. She was perfectly happy to send him a fucking CC email lying about her life, just to get rid of him.

What a total bitch.

Normally, he would let something like this slide. He would just not talk to her. He'd wait until she came back asking for his time and energy and ignore her like everyone else on his phone. But this was personal. He wanted to confront her about lying to him.

————

He'd tried to sleep, unsuccessfully, all night long. He stared over at where he'd woken to Christina the day before.

Fucking hell. I'm a mess.

He felt incredibly empty, and some of his initial anger had subsided. Maybe he'd overreacted some.

He didn't feel like working. For some reason, the feelings she aroused in him had returned. He wanted to finish that painting. He wanted to fill it with the colors of his heart and soul, to make sure it properly represented her. He made his way to the studio, ignoring Mr. Johannes' greeting and the sound of the post arriving. He just needed a few minutes of painting to clear his head before he dealt with anyone else.

Walking into his studio, he looked at her portrait. The same painting she didn't even know was her. She'd appreciated it. Seemed more interested in his work than he'd shown in hers. She may not have understood it at all. She may have complained about the mess in his room and been confused about how comfortable he was with the lack of cleanliness. But she hadn't tried to change it.

It was odd how her desire for order seemed to make her respect chaos. She was able to do so many things he was not able to do, and yet she respected when he did the opposite. Meanwhile, he admired only himself, only his own work, and sneered at those who tried to place some order in his life, as though they were the problem. However cold Christina had seemed, she had a sort of humanity, a sort of dignity about her that he could only dream of possessing.

But for all those abilities, she was unable to draw on people like he did, to make a friend, to hold down a relationship. For all the wealthy people in her life, none were her friends. He decided he should at least call her.

"Mia, call—fuck it, I'll do it myself."

Mia attempted to find a contact for "fuck it, I'll do it myself."

"Worthless piece of shit." He scoffed at the screen on the wall as he scrolled through the numbers in his phone and took a deep breath before tapping on hers.

The phone purred in his ear, and she didn't answer. Straight to voicemail.

He'd get to the bottom of this. He knew people.

———

Five hours later, he'd received a call and felt like an even bigger asshole. Not only was Christina's father basically terminal, the insurance company refused to pay his bills. Because he'd had the cancer before, the insurance had deemed it was a pre-existing condition and refused to cover his treatment.

The man Matty had called on was quite skilled. He'd hacked into Christina's accounts and done some online sleuthing. What he came back with hadn't surprised him. The medical bills were around forty thousand pounds. It was nothing to Matty. But, Christina had nobody with which she could call on for help. The amount would take all her savings to cover. It was merely a drop in the bucket to him, but she would be far too proud to ask him for help.

He knew Christina was capable of interacting with humans. She was just too proud or too stubborn to do it. Deep inside her eyes, he could tell that she wanted to be loved, and wanted a companion.

She was just really bad at accepting it.

Meanwhile, he craved order and structure. He needed it. He needed it so much that he'd tried to finish his father's design that would organize someone's entire life. He'd called in a professional to show him what he was doing wrong.

He wanted to follow schedules, to control his passions. He wanted to be orderly and disciplined.

He was just equally as bad at it.

Matty wanted to help her. And he would. It was his money, his life. Forty thousand pounds was nothing at all to him. It wasn't about passion, or emotion, or getting anything back. It was about the raw fact that he had more money than he needed, and she didn't.

If she was actively working at being passionate, the least he could do was try and be a bit more disciplined.

CHAPTER FOURTEEN

C hristina sighed and signed the bottom of the page at her father's rented house. She could repay the insurance company for their over-payments, cover her father's inpatient care, and have ten thousand left in savings for an emergency. How was it all disappearing so fast? She knew it was expensive, but none of this made sense.

Maybe she'd grown used to the NHS. Living most of her adult life with taxpayer-funded healthcare, the American forms confused her. Maybe she was too distracted by grief to notice any discrepancies. The insurance company was probably relying on her current mood to rip her off. She wouldn't put it past them. After reading the forms several times, all she could tell was that she would still have to pay roughly fifty thousand bucks for current treatments, and eight thousand for any in the future. So much for her savings.

It wasn't that bad, she thought. Her father wouldn't

be thrown out of the hospital and refused care. She was still young, after all. Her work in London paid well. She'd have the cash saved for her own place in another four or five years. The money was going to help her dad, and that was all that mattered.

She finished the paperwork and dropped it in her bag. Money meant nothing. Family was everything, even if she lived across the pond. Looking at herself in the mirror, she laughed. If only her hoity-toity clients could see her now—hair tied in a messy bun, leggings, wearing a faded maxi dress from the closet in her old bedroom. She actually looked her age for once. She sighed at the whole situation.

Being back home made her put her life in perspective.

Money.

It'd been controlling her. All of her clients cared so much about money. It was the reason they contacted her. And she cared so much about it that she put up with them, dressed for them, bent over backwards for them. All of it just to get some of her own. And now her father was ill, possibly dying at the hospital, and she hadn't come home to see him for several months. She felt like a piece of shit. Since when did money matter that much?

Her face broke out in a cold sweat on the way to the car. The money and bills wouldn't be a problem anymore. She didn't care if they both had to live in her studio apartment in the U.K. after this. She was scared of losing her father. She'd come straight to his house to drop off her stuff and was heading to go see him.

He'd been in horrible condition when he was first

diagnosed. The doctors had removed most of his pancreas and started him on a heavy round of chemotherapy. They did their best to push it back. It took three surgeries and three rounds of radiation before the samples came back cancer-free. By that point, his pancreas had been reduced to a fifth of its original size.

He had to learn how to eat differently. He was restricted by diabetes and couldn't digest fats. After a while, he put on a little weight and started to look healthier again. As soon as he was released from his first round of chemotherapy he made her leave to work and study. He knew how much her job and the country meant to her. He loved her and wanted her to have every opportunity in life. She returned to the U.K. shortly after.

He was the only person left who still loved her. If he died, she'd be all alone in the world again. Even worse off than when her mother passed.

She walked into his hospital room and was relieved that he didn't look near as bad as last time. But he'd lost weight again. His pallor was ashy gray. Skin hung off his cheekbones, and his eyes were purple from exhaustion. She hated seeing him like this.

She knocked lightly on his door. "Daddy. It's me."

His eyes lit up and he grinned. "Hey, sweetie. Was the flight okay? Jet-lagged?"

She tried not to burst into tears. He'd been in this condition and hadn't told her because he knew she'd come running back.

"I'm fine." She sat on the edge of his bed and hugged him. "I'm worried about you."

"It's no big deal. Caught it early this time. Already out. Another round of chemo and it'll all be gone."

Her heart hammered against her ribs. "And if it doesn't work?"

"More chemo, I think." His hand reached up and smothered hers. "It will. It's not like the first time. That damn thing had been growing for years. This one's small. I'll kick its ass."

She nodded and tried not to sniffle. "What did the doctors say?"

"Should be able to go home in a month or two."

Christina breathed a heavy sigh of relief. "I was so scared when they called. I-I thought—"

He wrapped his thin arms around her. "Sorry, baby girl. I didn't mean for them to scare you. You know how this shit goes, though. We stay strong and keep going. These problems just pass us by."

Christina looked away at the wall and wiped a tear from her eye. "They didn't pass Mom by."

His chin dropped to his chest. "No. They didn't."

She finally broke down. It was too much to hold in. She pressed her face into her father's chest and sobbed. "I th-th-thought I'd lost you."

Her father's arms tightened around her.

"Why would you think that? I've lived through worse than this."

"Because. You're so stubborn. You don't tell things until it's too late. I don't know if it's to try and protect me or what."

"Maybe. I just don't want you to miss any of your life on account of me."

She couldn't reply. All she could do was cry.

His arms squeezed her even harder. "I'm not going anywhere."

They stayed like that a few minutes and the tears finally stopped. She knew that her father wanted to cry, but she also knew that he would wait until she was gone. He was the same way the last time he got sick. He'd been the same way when her mom died too.

There was a knock at the door. "Sorry to interrupt."

Christina looked up. It was the doctor. She wiped her eyes, thankful she hadn't put on makeup.

"He needs to get some rest. You should probably come back tomorrow."

She nodded. They'd been kind enough to let her in at the end of visiting hours. She wasn't going to push her luck. "Thank you."

The doctor walked away, and she turned to her father. "Get some rest. I'll see you soon."

"Get some rest too. You look exhausted."

Leaving the room was hard, but she knew it was for the best.

Walking by the front desk, Christina remembered the forms and walked over. "I have some paperwork for Julio Smith. Copies of insurance forms and payment details."

"Great." The lady reached over and took the papers. Christina hovered, watching as the woman typed a few numbers into the computer.

"Julio Smith, birthday June seventh, nineteen fifty-eight?"

Christina nodded. A sudden panic came over her. "Is there a problem?"

"It's already been paid." The woman slid the paperwork back to Christina.

"I don't understand. I talked to the insurance company. They're not going to cover the upcoming fees, or the current ones." Just great. If they paid already she'd have to go back through everything and pay again, possibly with additional fees. It'd be a nightmare to keep track of.

"Not your insurance. It's from a private bank account. Did you pay this morning?"

"No. I just got into town and looked at the papers a few hours ago. Maybe someone made a mistake?" She didn't want to pay if she didn't have to. But she didn't want to deal with the charges if it was correct.

"It's definitely been paid. Let me have a look. A Mr. Spencer paid them this morning. There's a note on the file saying he'll handle all future billings. Is that correct? If it's not, I can have him refunded."

"Mr. Spencer? Is that from an overseas bank account?"

"Yes, it is. Do you know him?"

Christina hesitated. "Yes. I didn't think. Never mind, I'll get back to you."

"No problem. Have a nice day." She handed the bills and checks back to Christina.

She walked out of the hospital in a daze, slowly making her way over to the parking lot. She found her father's car. Forgetting what country she was in, she almost climbed into the right-hand side before she remembered and moved around to the left.

She sat down in the driver's seat and placed the forms on the steering wheel, and just stared at them in disbelief. He'd paid for it. He hadn't asked her for anything—hadn't sent her a message to brag or fish for compliments. There were no strings attached. He'd just paid it.

Nothing like this had ever happened to her before. Nobody had ever given her a handout. Nobody had ever been so kind to her. The closest thing she'd experienced to financial support was her student loan and healthcare back in the U.K. She'd never even had a friend pay for dinner. And now someone had paid fifty-eight thousand dollars for her, no strings attached.

She thought he wasn't anything special. Nothing more than another spoiled rich prick who didn't understand her life or her struggles. But even if he was, it didn't matter. He cared. For the first time in her life, someone other than her parents actually *cared* about her.

She stared up in the rearview mirror and noticed she was crying.

CHAPTER FIFTEEN

Matty looked at his online bank statement, making sure the payment had gone through. It was such a minuscule amount that the first three digits hadn't even changed on the balance. And that wasn't even his main account. He spent more than that when he wanted a new car, or when he invested in a company. It wasn't even enough to feel bad about. But it would mean so much to Christina.

It was confusing, but pleasing. He'd never really done anything like that for anyone else. He'd stared at his bank statement for most of the day. He couldn't fathom how something so small could make such a huge difference to someone. He couldn't make sense of someone needing so little money so badly. But if it helped her, if it made her life easier, then it would all be worthwhile.

He couldn't remember ever feeling so good about spending money.

It felt amazing—meaningful. What the hell. He could feel it again, so why not? And he knew exactly what he needed to do. There was something else that Christina wanted, something she'd been saving for.

He opened the website his friend had sent him. The house only had three bedrooms, one bathroom, a living room, and a kitchen. It was for her father.

He felt tempted to buy them something bigger, something better. In the sidebar, he saw similar places recommended nearby. Places with big yards, acres of land, and their own temperature-controlled pools. Places that were built in the last decade at least. Places with completely renovated kitchens, with five bedrooms, with hot tubs and skylights, and amazing home security features.

He was tempted to get her one of those instead. And even the most expensive one was only a million or so. It would be a noticeable expense, but nothing he couldn't make back in the next quarter. They would be well worth the money, too. Cheaper to run, nicer to live in. A much better place to raise kids.

Sure, maybe Christina couldn't afford anything better. But perhaps she would be pleased to find out that he'd bought her something more impressive?

He shoved away his thoughts. This was what she wanted. This was what she was saving up for. This was what she was always posting on social media about. It probably meant something to her, if she was so obsessed with this one little house. She was far too picky about things to go off and buy something ridiculous. He closed the other tabs and squinted at the pictures.

"Mia, call the number on the website."

As the number dialed out, he wondered briefly what the time was in Kentucky. He wasn't used to doing any of this. For all he knew it was the middle of the night over there. He caught the realtor at the end of her lunch break. At first, she sounded a bit annoyed, but after hearing she was about to make a sale with little to no effort, she changed her tune.

It felt odd to even be talking about that place. It was so far below his needs, so far below anywhere he would even set foot in. But it was what Christina wanted, so it was what she would get.

"We do have other places, you know?"

"Yes, I'm aware. I'm getting this for someone and she specifically asked for it."

"It has a lot wrong with it. Been on the market for nine years now with no offers."

He rolled his eyes. "Yeah, my friend wants it."

"Like I said, we have much nicer places, if you want to come and see them."

He sighed. Fucking realtors were always looking for a bigger commission, regardless of the country. "She asked for that one. It's that one or nothing."

There was a confused mumble from the other end of the phone. "Okay, just don't say I didn't try and tell you. Now, what are we doing about legal paperwork, keys?"

"I'm not sure. I've never bought someone else a home in another country before."

More confused noises emerged from the mobile,

followed by a brief, inaudible conversation with someone else in the room. "You need to be here."

"Do I really?" This was starting to be a lot of work, regardless of how much he liked her. He shook his head in frustration. No, he wanted to do it for her, so he soldiered on.

"Yeah, it'll make everything much easier with all the paperwork."

He sighed heavily. "Fine, I will go there for the legal side. But if I send you a straight payment for the house, can you at least send the keys along with a postcard to my friend?"

"Straight payment? As in, paying it all at once?"

"Yeah, sure. Plus a bonus for inconveniencing you. Say, ten thousand dollars?"

"That will be no problem, Sir."

He almost laughed. Christina would have a heart attack if she knew what he'd just done. She was wrong about one thing—it turned out that if you paid enough money, people really wouldn't question anything you did. Despite how long the earlier part of the conversation took, as soon as he started offering bonus payments she was very eager to secure the deal. People were so predictable.

He made the payment on the phone with her, before even signing the deal. He found himself snickering when she muttered something about foreigners and their strange ways. They agreed to meet two days later to finish everything, and the call ended.

He sat back in his chair, wondering what he even

expected to get out of this. It felt pretty good, but what could possibly result? Christina had made it abundantly clear that she wasn't interested in him as more than a client and a one-night stand. She also hadn't considered him important enough to tell him about her family situation. And having known her less than a week, he couldn't exactly claim he was entitled to anything else, emotionally or physically. The money was probably just going to vanish.

It didn't matter. He'd given her the money. He didn't expect to get anything for it. That was the way of these good deeds, he thought. It wasn't as if he needed anything anyway. He wasn't sure why he had lived his whole life blindly following the lessons his father had taught him. Spending money wasn't so bad. If she didn't appreciate it, then fuck her. It wasn't that much money. Technically, he could write it up as a bad investment and move on.

But, what if she came back? He stared at the wall. Nothing was being projected from his phone and still he wasn't quite sure where else to look. The room felt so empty. Why was his entire house so clean and empty and sterile, when he didn't even like it that way? Why did he bother living there and having dumb projections on his walls wherever he went just so he didn't feel like he was living in a box? He could easily afford to buy a beautiful cabin anywhere in the world and wake up with real birds and real sunshine, look out over a real lake or the sea, and fill his house with all the art he wanted to. Yet he'd spent all his money on an elaborate cage in a

London suburb, which he had enriched with artificial bollocks.

Perhaps he ought to fly to the USA that night, rather than the next day? Go and see her? But why? This wasn't a movie. She wasn't his Juliet or his Cinderella. They weren't living some amazing fairytale story of princes and paupers. And spending money on her would not make her fall in love with him.

If he showed up he'd probably be accused of being a creep. But who cared? He felt that they'd connected that night, and again the following day. There had been some affection, some understanding, the likes of which he'd never experienced before. And perhaps he was wrong. Perhaps she felt nothing at all for him and would be angry at him for showing up. But he would be angrier at himself if he didn't seize the opportunity.

"Mia, book me a ticket to Lexington, Kentucky."

"Booking one ticket from U.K., London, Heathrow, to U.S.A., Kentucky, Lexington, Blue Grass."

Christina was right. Mia was irritating even when she was working properly, and a serious problem when she wasn't. She couldn't replace a real human assistant like Christina. Not yet. And definitely not if he continued working on her design. He should leave things like this in the hands of people who knew what they were doing.

Speaking of not knowing what he was doing, he wondered what he would need to travel to Kentucky. He didn't know what the weather was like that time of year. What state laws he would have to think about, or anything else. But his flight was in three and a half hours, so he had to work it out quick.

This would be some kind of adventure. If she called him a creep and told him to fuck off, at least it would make for a nice holiday.

CHAPTER SIXTEEN

After waking up early, Christina slipped into her coat and tied her hair back. She made her way to the hospital, anxious to see her dad. The sooner she got there, the more time she'd have to spend with him before breakfast. Besides, she was used to getting up early for work.

Work.

If she didn't get back to London soon, there may be no work left. Mr. Spencer had paid for her dad, which meant less pressure, but she was still worried. She'd definitely need to get more clients soon, or she'd end up relying on others again, something she wanted to avoid. But she couldn't bring herself to leave for London until her dad was better.

She drove to the hospital and walked past the desk. The place was cold and smelled like Clorox. She knocked on her dad's door as she entered, then walked over to his bed.

She hugged him. "You look better today. I was pretty worried yesterday."

He nodded. "I always look worse in the afternoon. Don't worry so much."

"Can't help it."

"I just feel bad that you're spending money on me. Damn insurance should've covered this. You worked too hard on your savings."

"Actually, I didn't have to use any of it."

"What? The insurance people said they wouldn't cover anything. Bastards better not be trying to get us with more fees." He furrowed his brow.

Christina shook her head. "A friend of mine paid the balance."

Her dad's eyes widened. "All of them?"

She nodded. "All of them."

"That is a *lot* of money." He stared blankly. He'd never liked relying on others either. "We need to make a plan to pay her back somehow."

Her? She left it alone. She couldn't let her father know about Matty Spencer just yet. He was fiercely protective of her, and if he thought she was being taken advantage of by some British guy he didn't even know, he might go off the deep end. That was the last thing he needed right then. "I'll make sure."

"She must be rich as hell."

"Umm, yeah. She's very kind to do this for us."

"Don't lose that friend. She sounds like a good one."

Christina stifled a soft laugh. "Oh yeah." Yes, he was. He was chaotic and spoiled and confusing at times. But he was a good one, for sure.

"Did you bring the mail?" Her dad looked around for a bag.

"Shit. I forgot. Sorry, Daddy."

"Will you make sure to grab it on the next trip? The mail makes me anxious," he said. "And speaking of the mail, do you have any idea what this is?"

She took it from him. At first glance, it just looked like a picture of Lexington. But then she realized it was a postcard.

A postcard? Why the hell would someone send her a postcard from Lexington? To her Dad's hospital room?

Maybe it was some tourist thing. She turned it around and noticed it had the hospital's address with her and her father's names at the top. There was a key taped to it.

All it had written on it besides the address was "for your house" with an arrow pointing to the key.

She stared at the card for a few seconds, and then it all clicked at once. She made eye contact with her father. "Is this a joke?"

He shook his head. "That's what I thought. But it had both our names on it."

The house. It was the key to the house she'd been saving for. The one her mom had fallen in love with, that she wanted to buy for her dad. Christina collapsed in the chair beside her dad's bed. "I'm not sure I can take much more of this."

"Is it the same friend?"

"The postcard was sent from Lexington. I don't see how."

He shrugged. "Maybe she got someone else to send it?"

It was possible. This was all weird, hard to believe. Had he gone and bought her family a house? It wasn't a lot of money for him, but how could he have even known? And why would he bother? He was terrified of commitment.

"I have to check this out before we get excited."

She drove as fast as she could. This had to be some sort of a cruel joke, right? The place wasn't far out of town, but the drive felt like it took forever. It'd been a long time since she'd been there, but she managed to find it without any problems.

Her mother had always wanted the place. Always. Ever since she was a little girl, she remembered her mom asking for it. It was perfect. Memories all flooded in at once. It reminded her of where she'd been raised. Now, she could fix it up for her dad and they could make it their own. They'd never had the money to do it, and when her mom had passed away and her dad had developed cancer, Christina had committed herself to saving up and buying the place. It had meant so much to her mother, and she wanted her memory to live on. Even now, she felt like her mom was there with her.

Walking up to the door, she was too scared to try the lock. She'd got her hopes up too much.

Just then, a red rental car pulled up. It looked expensive, and she could barely make out the outline of the driver. She eyed it cautiously, even though she knew who it would be. How had he even managed to drive on the other side of the road? She laughed at the thought.

The door opened, and Matty stepped out, grinning ear-to-ear. He had bags under his eyes, five o'clock stubble, and was wearing a crumpled t-shirt.

"You look weird," he said. "Are you sure you're not Christina's cute little sister?"

She blushed bright pink and smiled. "I dress like this at home. At least I don't do it at work."

"Aren't you going to unlock the door?"

"Is this some kind of joke?" She raised an eyebrow. "Are you here to laugh at me?"

"Why the fuck would I come to Kentucky to play a joke? I could do that much cheaper in the U.K. Has nobody ever been nice to you before?" He walked up to the door beside her.

"No, not really." Her words were muttered, like a whisper.

"Here." He snagged the key from her hand, put it in the lock, and opened the door. "Your house."

She stared, wide-eyed, as the door slowly swung open. It smelled musty inside and the wallpaper looked like it was designed by hippies, but that didn't matter. "Is it really for my family?"

"Yeah, if it means so much to you. I can get you a nicer place, though, if you'd prefer. Somewhere a bit cleaner, a bit plainer."

She shook her head. "This is perfect. Seriously. It's perfect." She stepped inside, overwhelmed with joy and sadness all at once. This was the house her mother had always wanted. The house where her father could retire and relax as soon as his chemo was finished. He could live there in her mom's presence.

"How did you even find me? Or know about this house?"

He told her about his previous twenty-four hours. Went through everything.

He watched all her reactions, seemingly amused, as Christina walked around the house. She inspected everything. They both walked outside, and she stared up at the place once more. It was actually hers. After all these years. But she hadn't done it on her own.

"Why are you doing this?" She gulped and stared Matty in the eye. "I don't want to depend on you."

"I just wanted to give you a present. It feels good to give you things. I don't require anything in return, truly. Just take the gift." His eyes seared into her once more, like they always did.

"But why?"

Matty inched closer to her face, and her heartbeat kicked into overdrive. "Because I think I'm falling in love with you, and roses wouldn't cut it."

"I think I'm falling for you too." Her eyes stayed locked on his. "I thought you didn't want to get married, or do any of that stuff?"

"Oh, I don't. But, that doesn't mean I can't commit to you." He towered over her when she wasn't in heels.

She didn't take her eyes off him, though. She tried to look through and see if she could find the truth somewhere in his stare.

He leaned down and kissed her. Her breath hitched, and she noticed paint marks on his hands and face. She lifted her hand and gently stroked one on his neck. Mess and chaos. And it was wonderful. It was amazing to let go and be wild in the hands of a man as passionate and awesome as Matty.

He picked her up and sat her gently on the hood of the rental. For a moment, it felt wrong. They were outside. She was on top of a car. But she expected nothing less from Matty. He had that look in his eye again. Like he was hungry for her. This time it was different, though. He didn't look like she was a conquest. This time it was full of emotion.

"Why, Miss Smith, I do believe you want to get fucked on the hood of this car. Don't you?" He smiled.

"I knew your filthy mouth couldn't resist coming out to play at some point."

"It's in my nature. Hope you don't mind."

"I actually love it, to tell you the truth."

"That's good. Not that it would've mattered. If you're a good girl, maybe I'll spank that tight little ass of yours again." He pushed her skirt up as they kissed, bunching it around her waist, exposing her panties.

Her head shot around to make sure nobody was watching. "Matty Spencer." She smacked him on the shoulder. "Sorry I'm not wearing the stockings and lingerie you enjoyed so much last time."

He stared down at her Wonder Woman underwear. "I like you better like this." He smirked. "It suits you more."

"I rock everything I wear. And I'm not going to stop wearing business clothes because you like me like this."

"I think you forget one thing, love."

"What's that?"

He leaned over next to her ear. "You do whatever I say when we're about to fuck."

She gasped while he sucked down her neck. "Sorry, Sir. I forgot."

He yanked her panties aside and ran his fingers through her slick folds. "So fucking wet for me already."

She gasped and pushed back against his hand, her body practically begging for more of the delicious friction.

His lips pressed up against hers again and he unzipped his jeans, releasing his swollen cock she remembered all too well.

He looked around in both directions. "We'll have to be quick out here. I'll take my time with you later." Matty slid the head over the top of her clit, which coaxed a moan out of her. Then he smacked it a few times on top of her.

"Fuck." This time she cooed even louder. He felt amazing.

He knew how to tease her just right, like he'd studied her damn body his entire life. How did he do that?

He leaned back upright, and yanked her by the legs, spreading her simultaneously. It was rough and power-ful, and she could see in his face how fiercely he wanted her.

He teased her once more, pressing the head of his cock right up to her pussy.

"God, give me that dick already."

He pressed her legs back toward her shoulders with both hands, seemingly lifting her ass from the hood of the car. Then he let go with one hand and popped her right on the ass cheek.

"When I'm good and fucking ready, love."

"Jesus." Her head flew back onto the car, and she relished the stinging pleasure that radiated through her hips and legs. Maybe she should talk more shit to him? Get him really nice and fired up. There'd be a lifetime for her to test out that scenario, though. Right now, she just needed his hard dick inside her.

She lifted her hips as he guided himself in and hooked her legs behind his back. She dug her heels into his ass, trying to pull him deeper, but it really wasn't necessary. His hips quickly sped up until he was pounding into her, and she was screaming his name toward the forest off in the distance.

He was everything she wanted.

It didn't matter that this wasn't the right way to do things. It didn't matter that it was so soon, or so sudden. It worked for them, so why fight it? She'd always tried to plan her life out and it'd never worked out well. Maybe this spontaneity was what she needed?

His hand slid down, and he circled her clit while his cock pistoned in and out of her. She threw her arms up over her head and let go. Nothing but pleasure burst through her body. She tingled all over, and little sparks of electricity shot through her hips, and up her back, then out through all her limbs. She shuddered, convulsing, as her pussy clamped down on his cock.

He groaned and thrust one last time. She moaned when his cock twitched inside her, and he filled her full of hot come.

She ran her hands through his hair as he sucked her nipple lightly through her shirt. She could tell he was in love with her.

Before she knew what had happened, his cock was hard again, and fucking her just as relentlessly.

"Dear God, I've never had that happen before." He stared into her eyes. "Can't stop fucking this pussy, it seems." He grinned.

She pulled his hair, drawing him back up into a passionate kiss, and was once again on the verge herself. Jesus, she'd never had a man like this before. She clawed at his shoulders as she came on his cock for the second time in minutes.

He pushed deep into her one last time, her tight pussy gripping him, driving him over the edge. He moaned as he filled her up again. Feeling him explode inside her, she pushed down harder, desperate for every last drop. She came again—shivers running down her spine, while sparks danced behind her eyelids.

Regaining awareness of her surroundings, she realized his gaze was fixed on her, a smug grin on his lips. His body trembled a little, still supporting himself despite his exhaustion as he towered above her.

"How was that?" He waggled his eyebrows at her.

"That was the most irresponsible thing I've ever done in my life." She smiled.

"Was that an *actual* joke?" His grin widened. He pointed down at freshly fucked Christina with her skirt still hiked around her waist, and then stared around as if there were a crowd. "Hear that, ladies and gents? Christina Smith made a joke here today."

"Stop!" She smacked him in the chest, in a playful way.

"We shall have to memorialize the ground here."

She shook her head at him and smiled.

He leaned back down for a kiss. "I like making bad decisions with you."

As they kissed, she knew she was in the worst kind of trouble with Matty Spencer. It was all so sudden, all so fast—she barely knew this guy. But somehow, he was exactly what she needed. He was full of youthful energy, passionate, and spontaneous. They were complete opposites. He was the little spark she needed to embrace her feminine side. He was the motivation she needed to put up a fight, and the inspiration she needed to be herself. He was the primitive man that called her own cavewoman out to play. And she loved it.

It wasn't what she had ever truly imagined. It wasn't a childhood dream, or a carefully planned relationship. It was just what it was. And it worked.

Fuck the rules. Fuck order. They were meant to be.

EPILOGUE

Five Years Later

"I can't believe he's late." Christina held her eight-month pregnant belly as she whispered down at the baby. "This is not acceptable for you and your brother."

She half smiled. Christina couldn't remember being late for anything in her life, other than the two times that'd required a pregnancy test.

"Mommy, look at all the pictures."

"I know, sweetie. Aren't they great?" She reached down and took their three-year-old son, Carter, by the hand, and led him to the middle of the showroom. "Daddy is very talented. And in trouble for not being here to meet all these nice people that came just for him."

People walked around in tuxedos, and Christina felt

huge in her designer dress. Anxiety ran through her body. She wasn't equipped to entertain these people. Where was Matty? Was he in an accident? She'd checked her phone constantly for the past thirty minutes.

She and Carter made small talk with a few of Matty's friends and relatives.

She stared down at her watch before her gaze shifted to her ring finger. Still nothing on it. They were about to have their second child, and still, Matty hadn't asked her to marry him. It was okay. She knew he wasn't wild about marriage, and that it may never happen, but she was happy. She could work whenever she wanted, or not work.

And her life was great.

Christina still couldn't believe it was all real. Matty's first exhibit, or showcase, or whatever they called it in the art world. Rich buyers and critics were everywhere, admiring his work. Some of them for big-time newspapers published around the world.

Matty was still nowhere to be seen.

Only he could pull off being late to this shit.

She was going to kill him.

"Mommy, look! It's Papaw!"

Christina's heart came alive. "What?"

She whipped around to the front entrance. Matty pushed her dad through the front door in a wheelchair.

Dad still looked weak, but his smile stretched from ear-to-ear.

Her hand shot over her mouth. Tears welled in her eyes.

She hadn't seen him in a month. It was the longest stretch she'd gone without visiting her father in the past five years. After his last round of chemo, when Matty had bought the dream house, he'd gone back into remission. He'd beaten unbelievable odds time and time again for having pancreatic cancer. He was still weak, but they had nurses and the best medical care to look after him in Kentucky when they were home in the U.K.

She took Carter to see him once or twice a month and Matty went with them whenever he could. He seemed to like painting abstract versions of Lexington. Not to mention, he'd passed off the running of his father's company to his brother, who was actually capable of finishing Mia.

"How?" Christina stood there, clutching her mouth, trembling.

Her dad wasn't supposed to travel. He was too weak for the journey. But, he'd always told Matty he wanted to be there when he sold his first work of art.

"Mommy, you okay? It just Papaw." Carter took off running and jumped onto her father's lap.

Matty walked over, grinning from ear-to-ear. He moved her hands from her face and wiped the tears from her eyes. "Don't worry, love. He worked out hard for a few months, in secret, so he could make the trip over and surprise you. If you hate anyone, hate me for encouraging him."

She shook her head. "I don't hate you, I promise. This is—just—you know I'm pregnant, asshole." Christina smacked his shoulder, playfully.

"Ahh, yes, full of all the hormones and whatnot."

"I'm going to kill you."

Matty laughed. "Well, before you do, hold that thought."

He walked over, dressed in a pair of five-hundred-dollar jeans and a Rolling Stones tee-shirt, and grabbed a champagne flute and a fork off the refreshment table. He definitely looked the part of an artist.

Christina's dad rolled himself over to her and winked.

She started to talk, and he held up a finger. "I believe that boy's got something to say."

Matty clanked the fork against the glass. "Everyone, gather around, please."

"What are you doing?" Christina glared at Matty like he was out of his mind. "And who does that shit in real life?" She nodded at the glass he'd just clanked.

Matty smiled and set the flute and silverware aside. He walked over to her, slowly, but with purpose. His eyes narrowed, and his smile disappeared.

He turned to the crowd. "Thank you all for coming. Seriously, this is just—incredible. I'll let you get back to enjoying my doodles momentarily."

Snickers rang out at his joke.

"But, I have something that needs to be said. Christina is pregnant with our second child. This is her father. He's here from Kentucky. See, what happened was, I've had a question I've wanted to ask Christina for a very long time."

"Oh my God." Her hand covered her mouth once more, and her head began to spin. The tears welled up again, and she blinked them away.

"Carter, bring it over?"

Carter walked over in his mini tux, grinning the same grin as Matty. He looked like his father's twin, shrunk down to toddler size. He fished in the pocket of his too-big jacket and handed Matty a little blue box.

Matty smiled, clearly loving every second of torture he could inflict on Christina. She hated being the center of attention, but Matty reveled in it.

"I had to go all the way to Kentucky, ladies and gentlemen, to ask permission for what I'm about to do. And I couldn't very well ask this question, without Christina's father present. So, he's been working out hard, in order to make the trip over."

Oohs and ahhs rang out through the room when Matty opened the box and dropped down to one knee.

Christina felt like she might topple over, but she couldn't stop smiling and crying as she stared down at the same eyes that owned her that day when she walked into his mansion that was in complete disarray.

Matty's eyes fixated directly on her when he spoke, as if nobody else was in the room. "Y-you're—shit." He looked away.

Everyone in the room smiled as Matty choked up.

Christina let out a slight giggle. She'd never witnessed him at a loss for words like this. His face flushed with pink, and the hand holding the ring out to her trembled so hard she thought he might drop it.

"Excuse me. Sorry. Damn allergies."

More laughs.

Matty's eyes met Christina's once more. "You're everything." He swallowed. "My beginning and my end.

I'm not worthy of you, and I never will be. But, so long as I'm breathing and walking this planet, I will fight to be whatever you need me to be. Through anything. You're my heart. You're the mother of my children. You're my best friend, and when I'm with you, everything else fades away, and you and I are all that exists. You make me the happiest man alive, and I don't want the journey to end, ever. Christina Smith, will you marry me?"

Tears streamed down Christina's cheeks. She nodded furiously. "Y-yes!"

The place erupted in cheers, and Matty slipped the five-carat Tiffany diamond solitaire on Christina's finger. She stared at it, her eyes still blurred with tears, while Matty wiped them away.

"How? How does it fit?"

He leaned down to her ear. "I had them size it up until after the pregnancy, and then we'll have it resized after the baby comes." His hand landed on her belly.

"But, but, how did you even know to do that? I never mentioned my fingers being swollen."

"I pay attention, love. I know everything about you. And I always will."

They kissed, long and hard to the sounds of cheers and people shouting "congratulations!"

When they parted, she walked over and gave her father a hug. He shook Matty's hand.

"Thanks for bringing me over here in style."

"No problem, Sir. Couldn't very well have you miss this."

"This is some place. I'm proud of you, Son."

"Thank you, Sir. I'll leave you two to it th
the boy have got to go work the room,
Carter?"

Carter nodded, and his face lit up with a smile.

Matty scooped him up and carried him around,
pointing to paintings and talking to random people
about his artwork

Christina had been worried when she first found out
she was pregnant with Carter. She'd had no idea what
type of father Matty would be.

Turned out, she didn't need to worry about it at all.
He loved that boy more than anything. He loved his
whole family more than anything in the world.

So that was why he'd waited so long to ask.

Even five years after meeting, he could still surprise
her every day.

"How long are you here for, Daddy?"

"Matty says as long as I want. It's a little cold and
rainy, but they fry up some good fish around here.
They call the fries chips, though. You believe
that shit?"

Christina snickered and hugged him once more.
She'd always wanted her dad to visit, but he'd been
so sick.

"How's the house?"

"Great. A little lonely sometimes when you guys
aren't there, but I make do. There's always a nurse or
someone stopping by. I've been reading a lot, and guess
what? I had a date last week."

"What?" Christina made a show of asking the question, and her mouth dropped open, clearly teasing him.

"I know it. Been working out for this trip. Apparently, getting ripped is the secret to attracting women."

"Jesus, Dad."

He chuckled.

Christina shook her head at Matty, and her hand slid over her father's thin fingers. It was the best day of her life, by far. "I can't believe he was late for his first show."

"Yeah, we got caught in some traffic."

She shook her head again and turned back to her dad. "I guess he had a pretty good reason. I'll let it slide this time."

She bent down and hooked her arms around her dad's neck and kissed him on the cheek. "I love you."

"Ohh, I love you too, sweetie. I'm just glad that you're happy. It's all your mom and I ever wanted for you."

Her hand cradled her stomach once more, and she smiled at Matty and Carter. "I am. I really am."

Flip the page for a sneak peek into other works by Alex Wolf

CHAPTER 1

Tom

"Thank you so much for this opportunity, Mr. Carver."

"Call me Tom. And I'm happy to do it. When Hannah said you were looking for an internship, I knew this would be a perfect opportunity, for *both* of us."

Her chest blooms pink, and it spreads up her neck to her cheeks. Rose is my daughter's college roommate. I couldn't say no to Hannah. I've always spoiled her, and she knows all she has to do is ask and it'll be done

"I'll work hard. You won't regret this, I promise."

Yeah, you will.

"You sure I won't bother you? I know you're super busy. I don't want to get in your way." She shifts in her seat, crossing her ankles.

My eyes dart down to a pair of fuck-me heels, and my gaze rakes up her lean legs. Inappropriate things race through my mind every time I see Rose Collins. I know it's wrong, but fuck, she's hot.

"Not at all. You're staying at the apartment over the break, and we'll be working a lot of hours. You'll be sick of me in no time."

"That'll never happen." She glances out the window. "I can't believe Hannah's going to Europe with Steven for the summer. I'm going to get lonely." She flashes me a weak smile and straightens up in her chair. "I don't party or anything like that. I want you to know that I'll take my position seriously."

You won't be lonely. Trust me.

"I doubt that. You'll have men falling at your feet. I already noticed a few staring on the way in. We'll keep you busy, though. Lots of work to do around here."

I'll keep you busy.

"You're just trying to make me feel better." She takes off her glasses as she finishes her new-employee paperwork.

I will definitely make her *feel* better. God, she has no idea how sexy she is. Legs for days. Dark hair pinned back neatly. Hair I'd love to yank on and run my fingers through. Soft red lips that'd look perfect wrapped around my cock as I fucked her mouth. And those tits. *Fuck.* She's nothing but walking temptation.

I stare hard into her hazel eyes. "I don't lie. I mean *everything* I say."

"Well, umm, I should let you get back to work. Unless you want me to start today."

"Actually, I do need you. I have a meeting, and my assistant is on maternity leave. Can you take notes? I have some other errands you could take care of as well."

You could take care of my rock-hard cock.

Her eyes lock onto mine. A wry smile curls her lips upward as she nibbles the end of her pen. I can't help but imagine that tongue of hers swirling around the head of my dick.

"Sure. Anything you need."

Anything?

"Could you grab a file for me? It's right behind you."

"Sure." She caps her pen and sets it beside the paperwork.

Her dainty fingers smooth down her skirt. They should be on me, stroking up and down my shaft while she awaits further instruction.

I shouldn't think these things, but I can't help myself.

She's beautiful, smart, tempting—and, not to mention—forbidden. Which makes me want her even more, considering I'm a man who always gets what he wants.

"Bottom drawer. File titled 'Titan Industry'."

My eyes dart to her ass as she bends down to get the folder. Her charcoal gray skirt hugs her soft curves in all the right places. I want nothing more than to bend her over my desk, dig my fingers into her, and sink my cock deep inside her tight virgin pussy.

Rose is a good girl. I overheard her and Hannah before Hannah left for her trip.

Hannah had said, *"Don't be uptight all summer. Get drunk or, I don't know, lose your virginity."*

Fuck, just hearing she was a virgin had my cock warring with my zipper. Rose needs a man to guide her, teach her things. A real man. Not some fucking frat-boy loser. She dated some clown all semester who cheated on her because she refused to give it up. Motherfucker didn't deserve her.

Not that I do, but I'm exactly what she needs.

Not some little cocksucker who treated her like shit and made her cry.

I have to do this right. If I move too fast, I'll scare her off. I have no doubt by the time I make my move, she'll be begging for it.

Her fingers brush over mine as she hands me the file. It shocks me out of my thoughts. Her touch is electric. It pulses through my limbs.

"Thank you." I smirk when her cheeks flush with pink hues.

I'm going to enjoy this—playing with her.

"Is there anything else I can do, Mr. Carver?"

The way she says my name drives me fucking crazy. I know I told her to call me Tom, but she just changed my mind.

Right now, I want nothing more than to swipe everything off my desk, sit her on top of the hard oak, and eat her pussy for lunch.

"I was about to get some food. Why don't you order us something?"

"What do you want?"

Your legs, trembling around my face. Now.

My eyes roll up to meet hers. "Surprise me."

Her teeth sink into her bottom lip. "Okay."

CHAPTER 2

Rose

I have no idea what to order him for lunch.

I've been around Mr. Carver a few times, but never enough to pay attention to what he eats.

Men like meat and sandwiches, I suppose. I decide to order him a club and fries. I opt for a burger. My stomach grumbles a little at the thought. I'm freaking starving. I was too nervous to eat breakfast.

I want to do my best to make a good impression here.

If I do well, maybe they'll offer me a job when I graduate. A low, entry-level job, but it would be an awesome start.

Carver Global would be an amazing company to work for.

I sit in his office and watch him devour the sandwich

while I pick at my burger. Apparently, I chose well. I can't help but be intrigued by the man in the suit.

He lets his guard down, and laughs. Ketchup drips down his chin. Without thinking, I take a napkin and wipe it away.

When he smiles, my heart drums in my chest.

His hand reaches out and covers mine. "This was perfect. Thanks."

"You're welcome."

"You do this every day, I may have to keep you around permanently."

His tone is light, but his stare smolders me. God, he looks like he could throw me over the desk and do unspeakable things to me. Every time he talks—*Jesus*. He's powerful, experienced, charming—and just too fucking hot for words.

———

I step out of the shower, and my body welcomes the cool air. Today couldn't have gone better. I spent most of it running errands for Mr. Carver. I really should call him Tom like he requested. It's just that I've always known him as Hannah's dad.

He's the president of a multi-billion-dollar company. Calling him by his first name seems so—I don't know— informal or insulting. Maybe I'm making a big deal out of nothing. My mind does that sometimes. But the man just oozes power and sophistication. I've never seen a more gorgeous man for his age. He could be a model for Dior.

Thinking about how he looked in his office today, how he looked at me, it sends a tingling sensation between my thighs. I could swear a few times when he looked at me, there was something between us.

I shouldn't think about him like this, but I can't stop myself.

The man is fine.

A real silver fox. His eyes are steely grey and penetrate my core like armor-piercing rounds. And his smile —fuck, his smile.

I walk over to my door and crack it open, barely. I don't think he's home from work yet.

I stroll over to my nightstand, open the top drawer, and pull out my B.O.B.

I can't get Tom's searing eyes out of my mind, and I need to release this tension before it destroys me.

Biting my lip, I drop my towel and lie down on the bed.

My fingers trail over my breasts, caressing my nipples, imagining my hands are his.

It's not the first time I've gotten off to the thought of Tom Carver. It's even more intense now, knowing I'm staying at his apartment. It's like his presence is all around me. He's been in this room, probably sat on this bed. He could be home any time.

The first time I met him was a party at their house in the Hamptons. We arrived early, and he was out by the pool. He definitely works out and takes care of himself. He's muscular but not overly thick. He has a trim build, like a swimmer's frame, and that damn vee that cuts down below his shorts. It took everything I had not to gawk with my mouth wide open.

Arching my back and spreading my thighs, I circle my fingers over my clit. My body burns with need. There's an ache between my legs that only thoughts of Tom can heal.

It's too bad I can't have him.

Spreading my fingers through my slick folds, my pussy is ready for B.O.B. to do his job.

I power him on and glide him inside while fantasizing about my new boss—my best friend's dad.

I work it in and out, the entire time imagining it's Tom's thick cock pumping in and out of me.

I've fooled around before, and I have B.O.B., but I've never been with a man.

I came close with my ex, but found out he was cheating on me. It was actually a relief, even though I cried myself to sleep for a week. Thank God I didn't give him what he wanted before I found out.

I'm saving myself for someone I can trust.

A man who knows what I need and won't shatter my heart into a million pieces.

A man like Tom Carver.

I'm so close to finding my release when I hear a door close. I yank the covers up over my body.

"Rose? You eat dinner yet?"

Oh my God.

B.O.B.'s vibrations and the sound of his voice sends me over the edge, and my eyes roll up in my head.

A knock on my door sends it wide open.

I freeze, legs spread on my bed, completely exposed

beneath the covers, and in walks the man I can't stop thinking about.

The orgasm rolls through my body, which moves on its own accord. My hips buck as his eyes narrow on me.

There's no way he doesn't see what I'm doing. Well, what I *was* doing.

Jesus, I could die right here on the spot, but it feels so fucking good.

Tom doesn't move or speak, but a tiny muscle jumps in his cheek, and his chest heaves and falls with each breath. He's lost the jacket of his suit. His button-down stretches tight across his broad chest, tie loosened around his neck. His hungry eyes sear into me.

What the hell am I going to do?

Does he know I was thinking about him? Does he know I want nothing more than for him to close the distance between us and fuck me?

CHAPTER 3

Tom

Fuck, it's impossible to concentrate at work with Rose nearby. She has no idea what she did to me earlier in that meeting. While I was negotiating the terms for a new contract, all I could focus on were those tempting lips. The way she nibbled the tip of her pen nearly drove me over the edge. I was on the verge of throwing everyone out of the room and bending her over the conference room table.

I've never felt this way before, and I've had my share of women.

I don't know what it is about her, but I can't get her out of my head.

I canceled a client dinner to try and catch her before she ate. I want to spend as much time with her as possible, get to know everything about her. I want her underneath me, coming on a scream, while her pussy clamps around my cock.

When I get home, I catch her in her room and can't believe my eyes. It's like winning the lottery.

Pure, innocent Rose, on the bed, toying her sweet little cunt with a vibrator.

The primal urge to shove my cock into her rages through my body.

She's frozen. A deer in the headlights.

"Don't stop on my account."

"Mr. Carver, umm, I—"

Embarrassment rushes into her cheeks, but her eyes tell a completely different story.

Doesn't she know she's playing with fire, and I have absolutely no problem watching her burn?

"I told you. Call me Tom." I walk to the side of her bed, confidence in each of my steps.

She's beautiful, and my cock hardens, imagining what her body looks like under the covers.

Her eyes sparkle while she waits, and I can tell she's still touching herself as she looks at me.

I pride myself on being able to read situations, but I hadn't expected her to be this naughty so soon.

My fingers brush along her jaw and over her lips. Her warm breath plays across my hand.

Her tongue darts out, tasting the tip of my thumb, while her eyes seem to ask for permission.

Fucking Christ.

I flash her a devilish smile. "Well, well, aren't you just full of surprises."

Her eyes widen as she holds my gaze. "Mr., umm,

Tom, I-I don't know what came over me. I don't know why I just did that." She looks away.

I shove a finger in her mouth. "I think I like you calling me 'Mr. Carver' better."

Her cheeks suck around my finger, and her tongue swirls around it. I can't help but imagine what it'd feel like, her doing the same thing to my cock.

Soon.

"So, what should we do about this? Do I need to take you over my knee? Punish you for being a dirty little bitch in my house?"

She moans around my finger when she hears my words. "If you think that's what's best—"

I stare down at her.

Her eyelashes flutter. "*Mr. Carver.*"

"Hmm." I make a *tsk-tsk* sound and decide I'm going to take my time with her. Break her pussy in just right. Mold it to my cock. "I was going to invite you to dinner. I'm fucking starving." I reach down and fist the back of her hair.

Her eyes fly open, and then fall half-hooded.

I lean down next to her ear, careful to exhale into it. "But you'll be so much better."

Her eyes close. "Oh my God," she whispers.

I unbutton my shirt and peel it from each arm right in front of her. She looks like she wants to jump from the bed and attack me. But she knows better. It's very clear who's in charge right now.

Rose's gaze stays fixed on me as I strip bare. Her tongue pokes slightly through her lips as I take my pants down. I smirk when she gets her first look at my cock. Her eyes turn into saucers.

My dick's so hard it hurts. There's nothing in the world I've ever wanted more than to feel her tight little cunt milk every last drop from it. I need to taste her first, though.

I hook a finger under the covers near her neck. "You sure?"

She nods.

I drag them slowly down her body as I speak. "You can decline. But we both know that's not going to happen." Fucking hell, the sight of her naked is almost too much to bear. Light pink nipples, pussy shaved bare —it takes everything I have not to groan or growl, something. She's so fucking hot my mind goes blank. Functioning becomes difficult. "Tell me the truth, Rose. What were you doing?"

"I-I was thinking about you."

"I know." I trail a finger up her inner thigh, right next to her pink, wet pussy. "Did you ask permission to play with *this* pussy, in *my* house?"

"Oh my God." Her words are a whisper as her eyes close. "N-no. I'm sorry."

"Something has to be done about this."

"Whatever you want." She lets out a light gasp.

Jesus.

I lean up to her face and claim her with a kiss. Her lips part immediately. She doesn't dare to fight against me. She lies there as I take whatever I want. Our tongues mingle and explore—licking and sucking.

Fuck, she tastes so damn sweet.

I reach down and toss her vibrator to /
"Won't be needing that." I lick down her throat ᴜ.
smile against her neck. "You have no idea how good I'm
going to make you feel."

I slide my hand down to her inner thighs and shove
her legs apart. She moans, and her hands fly back above
her head, gripping the pillow.

I can't help but smile at the way she reacts to every
motion, every action of mine. I hold a power over her,
and it turns me on damn near as much as her tight little
body. I brush my thumb over her clit, just to watch her
shudder. She's so close, already on the edge of release.

This is going to be fun.

Her tight cunt pulses with need as she rocks against
my hand.

I lean up slowly to her face, as if I might kiss her,
and then turn so my mouth is right in her ear. Roughly, I
cup her virgin pussy in the palm of my hand and
squeeze. "This is *mine*. Understand?"

She can't nod her head fast enough.

You can get your FREE ebook of Banging the Intern by
visiting https://dl.bookfunnel.com/j017mcu2ao

PROFESSOR'S PET SNEAK PEEK

CHAPTER 1

"Fuck!"

Kristen flew out of bed.

What the hell happened?

Her brain was a dense fog for a moment before she realized instead of hitting the snooze button she'd turned the alarm off. She hopped on one foot and pulled her jeans on, then yanked a shirt over her head. She'd planned on getting up early and spending an hour in front of the mirror, fixing her hair and makeup for class. Staying out until one in the morning drinking hadn't been the wisest decision the night before.

A few of the girls she'd met during orientation convinced her it was a good idea. She didn't want to be known as the square, studious girl who lived her life in the library. She had to make a good first impression and turning potential friends down on the first day wouldn't be the best way to start off.

One drink soon turned into ten. They'd promised

Kristen they'd only be out for an hour or so, and before long it had morphed into an all-nighter. By the time she'd crawled into bed, she was seeing double and the ceiling danced around her head.

"Fuck me."

She scolded herself in the mirror, grabbed her hair, and yanked it into a loose bun. Her hands were a blur as she lined her eyes and dabbed on some shadow, hoping it would disguise the hangover. When she bent over to tie her shoes, nausea slammed into her stomach, and her heart beat on her temples. It was going to be a rough first day.

Normally, she'd have chosen to pair her jeans with boots or sandals, but given her predicament, she didn't have much time to think, let alone select a good outfit. She also wasn't certain she had everything in her backpack, but it'd have to do. She sprinted out the door of her dorm room and into the hall.

Of course, if she'd been on time, there would've been far more students in the halls, but since she was already half an hour late, the building looked like a ghost town.

"Shit. Shit. Shit." She mumbled her words as she dashed down the stairs and ran across the lawn. Each step was like someone pounding her skull with a sledge-hammer. Crowds of other students hung in small packs, and some of them stopped and stared as she flashed past them. Others ignored her completely.

Kristen wasn't in the mood to talk anyway, nor did she really give a shit what they thought about her. She'd made a mistake the night before. She quickly realized she didn't want to be popular. She came to get her degree, and that was what she was going to do.

I'm never drinking again.

She stopped a guy who looked like a senior. Surely, he'd know where her class was.

"Journalism 101?" She bent over at the waist, panting while she waited for a reply. She knew the general direction of where she was supposed to go, but she didn't want to waste any extra time. The guy looked her over from head to toe with a smirk. He clearly enjoyed the fact she was lost and wanted help. What was it about men that made them love a helpless female? His eyes roamed her chest before shifting back to her face.

Kristen crossed her arms and raised an eyebrow. She let out an obvious sigh, making it a point to look unimpressed.

"First day?" He grinned. Apparently, he liked what he saw.

She tilted her head to the side. "Obviously."

He laughed. "Go around the corner. First door on the left." He pointed in the general direction.

She took off.

"Better hurry. Not cool to be late, freshman. Even if you're hot."

As she rounded the corner, she couldn't help but think how annoying college guys would be. She had no intention of hooking up with any of the boys on campus, and that's what they were—boys. Nothing would jeopardize her future. The last thing she needed was to get involved with some jock who might knock her up and vanish.

She intended to have fun, but she wasn't about to fuck the first guy she saw in the hall to accomplish the goal. The dude was cute, but she shuddered a little at the fact he stared at her tits before answering her question.

Asshole.

She reached the door to her class and paused for a deep breath.

This is it.

She shoved the door open and walked into the room. Aspirations of being a journalist meant this would be one of her most important classes. That's why she scheduled it first thing in the morning. Normally, she was a morning person and got most of her work done before lunch.

If things had gone according to plan, she'd have been there an hour early, not hauling ass at the last second.

Get your shit together, Kristen.

She kept her head down and hurried to a seat in the back. Maybe it wouldn't be so bad. Maybe the professor wouldn't even notice her. She was there now, and if he did catch her, she'd just apologize and tell him it wouldn't happen again.

There was only one problem.

The door made a god-awful squeak that echoed off the walls, and it closed with a loud clank before suctioning shut. All of this before she'd even found her seat.

Shit.

Everyone in the damn class turned and stared. She

didn't care what her classmates thought. It was none of their damn business. At least she made it to class at all, which she was sure would be a chore for some students.

Fortunately, the professor had his back to her. She breathed a sigh of relief, until he stopped writing on the board. Kristen kept her eyes on the floor as she slinked through the back of the room. She took a seat in the last row and avoided all the stares as if nothing had happened.

The chair was like nails on a chalkboard against the tiled floor when she pulled it out. She winced.

Son of a bitch.

Everyone stopped what they were doing, even the professor, as if time had suddenly stood still and she was the only one moving. It wasn't until the room was completely silent again that the professor resumed teaching.

His voice boomed when he spoke. "*As* I was saying, the most important thing you can know as a journalist —" He turned around and glared at Kristen, but her head was angled down toward the desk.

She could see him in her peripheral vision and practically feel the heat of his gaze on the top of her head.

"Is that you have to be *on time.*" He turned back and scribbled on a dry-erase board while he continued. "If there's a story, the sooner you get it into the public's hands, the better. Good journalists don't just get a story, they get it first."

Her cheeks burned and heat rushed into her face.

Maybe he'd been talking about being on time before

she'd walked through the door, she thought. She could hope anyway.

"What does that have to do with those of us who aren't going to be journalists?" another student asked.

"Punctuality will serve you well in life, regardless of your field of practice. You will learn plenty of principles in this class that will prepare you for the world. Keep an open mind, and you may be surprised where you end up."

Kristen kept her eyes trained on the syllabus someone had passed her. She was uncertain how much of the lecture had to do with her or if she was being paranoid.

Even though she'd shown up to the class late, she still felt it dragged on for the rest of the period. Maybe it was the fact she wanted to speak with the professor about being late—set things straight—or maybe she didn't find Intro to Journalism as interesting as she'd thought it'd be.

Either way, seconds turned into minutes, and minutes turned into an hour. She just wanted out of the class and back to her dorm room. She silently prayed that interaction would be minimal the first day, and she could start over new tomorrow.

Finally, class came to an end, and the professor dismissed them. Kristen had stared down the entire time and pretended to take notes, afraid to look up again, worried her professor would notice her bloodshot eyes. Now that it'd ended, Kristen decided she'd face her fear. Walk up and apologize for being late and assure him it wouldn't happen again. It was the adult thing to do, and she was in college now.

After a few stragglers made their way to the door, she headed up to his desk.

"Excuse me, professor."

Her heart thumped in her chest, and she could still feel it beating in her head. Kristen had always dealt with anxiety to some extent, and now that she stood in front of her professor, she worried he might take off points for being late.

"I just wanted to apologize. I didn't mean to be late. My alarm didn't go off. I got here as soon as I could." Her chest constricted, and she thought she might be having a heart attack.

"I'm not interested in excuses."

She looked away. She hadn't meant to make excuses. In fact, in her mind it wasn't an excuse, just a reason. How did he not understand that? It was the first day. She'd never been there before. She could've been lost. Maybe she misjudged the distance to the building. It wasn't true, but he didn't know that.

"Well, I just wanted you to know it won't happen again." She forced a smile.

He still hadn't looked at her, and she worried he wasn't listening.

"This class is absolutely a priority for me. You don't have to worry about this again."

God, you already said that. Just go. You sound like an idiot.

"It's not me who has to worry. And if it's a priority, where were you this morning?" He finally looked up from his desk.

She started to speak, but the words caught in her throat. Her breath hitched. She noticed his eyes first—icy blues that seared into her. Her mind went blank, and words refused to form in her brain.

He was by far the most attractive man she'd ever seen.

He let out an exasperated sigh. "You won't be penalized this time. Don't let it happen again."

CHAPTER 2

Kristen clutched her books to her chest as she walked back to her room. She noticed other students staring, and a few even greeted her as she passed. Nothing registered, though. She couldn't get her professor out of her mind.

Professor Grant Wiseman was the hottest man she'd ever met in her life. It made the whole situation worse.

She knew he was smart, and it was probably easy for him to deduce that she was hungover. If her eyes didn't give it away, she probably still reeked of booze.

She wished the ground would open up and swallow her whole. Maybe then she'd be able to get the professor out of her head. Grant was tall, even when sitting down. He looked in his late thirties. His hair was jet black with dashes of silver mixed in—salt and pepper. He kept the sides trimmed low, and the longer hair on top slicked back. And, Jesus—the glasses. He wore dark-framed spectacles that were the sexiest pair she'd ever seen, coupled with the icy-blue irises that sat behind them.

He clearly worked out, the way he filled his dress shirt, and despite being quite a bit older than her, he was still lean and fit. There had to be some story behind him teaching journalism at California State University, and she wanted to know what it was. During their interaction, she'd forced her mind to think of anything other than his body, and by the time they'd finished their little talk, she could barely recall any of the conversation.

All she'd taken away was she'd gotten off with a warning. She wouldn't mind getting off with more than that in the presence of the hot professor. She'd rushed from the room shortly after. The last thing she wanted was to make the situation any worse than it already was, and she knew she was on thin ice. Professor Wiseman didn't seem like the kind of man who allowed his students to be late, ever.

There would definitely be no shortcuts in his class.

"How'd it go?" Stefani, her roommate, turned to Kristen as she walked through the door of their room.

"Why didn't you wake me up?" Kristen knew it wasn't Stef's job to get her out of bed, but she also knew she was probably up around the same time.

"I didn't know you had class. You were out late. I figured you had afternoon classes today." Stefani shrugged. "Sorry."

Kristen sighed and threw her books on the bed, then sat down in a chair, rubbing her temples. "I was thirty minutes late, and the class is only an hour and a half."

"Sorry. If I'd known, I would've given you a good

shake." Stef typed something out on her laptop as she spoke, then turned to look at Kristen. "How you feeling?"

"Don't apologize. It's not your fault I'm an idiot." Kristen sighed. "I feel like shit. Hungover. And get this. I had the hottest professor of all time."

Stefani spun around in her chair. "Really? Tell me more."

Kristen nodded and told Stef everything that happened on the way into class.

"Well, just be on time from now on. Shouldn't be a big deal. He'll notice you putting in the effort. Everyone makes mistakes."

She smiled at Stef doing her best to cheer her up. "Thanks."

Judging by Stef's cheery demeanor, there was no doubt her day had gone far better.

Oh well, there was nothing she could do about it now. She grabbed her books and climbed onto her bed to take care of her homework.

Daydreams of Professor Wiseman quickly invaded her thoughts and took over. Different scenarios and how she'd affected his opinion of her played through her mind. She overanalyzed everything, and often dwelled on the tiniest details and actions.

How could a man like that end up at a school like this? Was he really pissed at her for being late? And then there was the most important question, what did he think of her?

"You're up. Good. I was about to start jumping on your bed." Stefani finished a bowl of cereal and stared over at Kristen, who was sitting up in her bed.

Kristen had set several alarms the night before, bound and determined to get up on time. After Wiseman's class, and the entire next day, she'd made it a point to not be late again.

"Thanks, but no way was I going to be late twice in a row." She shook her head and snickered. Her nerves had kept her up most of the night. She was worried she'd sleep through her alarm again.

"Good luck." Stef headed out the door.

Kristen threw the blanket off her legs.

Since she was up on time, she could be a bit more selective in choosing an outfit.

She flipped through her closet, trying to decide what to wear. Normally, she'd just grab something comfortable, more concerned about what she was going to do with herself that day than how she looked while she did it. That was before she had someone to impress. Today, Kristen only had one thing on her mind that seemed to guide her wardrobe selection.

Professor Wiseman.

She wanted something that would get the professor's attention and show off her tightly toned body.

She wasn't sure why she was dressing up for him, but she couldn't help herself. She settled on a pink mini skirt. It was cotton and barely covered her ass. It definitely highlighted every curve and left little to the imagination. Her father had hated the skirt, and more than once sent her back to her room when she'd tried to go out in it, but like every teenager, she'd insisted on keeping it. She hid it from him and wore it only when she knew he wouldn't find out.

She wasn't sure why she'd brought it to college with her because she had no intention of ever wearing it. But she now found herself grateful that she did. Pairing it with a tight tank top, she figured it was enough to make the professor drool a little.

Instead of pulling her hair up into a bun again, she took the time to put curls in it, then finished her look with some eyeliner and mascara. With each stroke of the brush, she thought more and more about Professor Wiseman and what he would think when she walked into the room.

Once she approved of herself in the mirror, she grabbed her things and headed out of the dorm.

There was plenty of time to get to class, but it was difficult to hold herself down to a casual walk. Her heart thumped with each step toward the building, but this time without the headache and nausea.

She was enjoying the little fantasy in her mind when she entered the classroom and what he would think of her outfit when he noticed. He probably wouldn't say anything at all, but then again, he wouldn't have to. Those icy blues would tell her everything she wanted to know.

In the corner of her eye, she could see guys gawking as she passed. She smiled to herself and put a little sway into her hips as she continued toward the building, knowing with each step she took they all fantasized about what they'd like to do to her.

When she finally got to class, she once again hesitated and took a deep breath before walking inside.

Why was she so damn nervous? He was just a man.

Unlike the last time she was in the class, she didn't avoid eye contact with anyone. Kristen squared her shoulders and strode through the door, smiling at the boys who dared to look her way. Kristen had never lacked confidence, and it only grew when she saw the way the other students reacted.

When she was in high school, she'd deliberately do things to draw attention to herself, and now that she was in college, she didn't plan to change.

The only person she didn't make eye contact with was Professor Wiseman. Her palms grew slick as she walked across the room, purposefully taking her seat at the front. When she sat down, she looked up at him with a broad smile.

The second his eyes met hers, he quickly looked away.

A little thrill of triumph ran through her body and landed between her legs.

He cleared his throat and gathered the papers on his desk. It seemed he had a difficult time keeping his attention on his work instead of staring at her. Each time he'd glance over to the class, he'd make it a point to not look at her, and each time he did have to look at her, he stared directly into her eyes.

She smiled once more after class let out. "Made it on time, professor."

He glanced up and locked eyes with her, not daring to look down at her body.

"Are you looking for a pat on the back for being on time?" His attention moved back to the papers in front of him. His voice was harsh and cold.

"No, sir. Just making conversation."

What an asshole.

He still hadn't tried to check her out, either. What the hell?

She rose from her seat and made a show of bending over right in front of him to pick up her books. The cool air tickled the backs of her thighs, and she knew her panties were alarmingly close to being visible. She wondered if she made his cock thick and hard under the desk.

Kristen wanted to glance back and watch his reaction, but it'd be too obvious. She purposely fumbled around with something in one of the books, so that she could linger a bit more. He'd definitely be jerking off to her later.

When she stood, he pretended to ignore her.

"See you Friday." She walked toward the door.

She desperately wanted to stay and chat, see how uncomfortable she could make him, but she didn't have any questions about the class, and she wanted to remain a mystery. Everything had gone perfect, and she didn't want to ruin it. She'd leave and go back to the dorm before her next class, but it was impossible to get him out of her mind.

She was the last one out the door, and she swore she'd heard a groan right before the door closed.

She was obsessed.

It was going to be a long semester.

CHAPTER 3

Grant breathed a sigh of content when he walked through his front door. It'd been a long fucking day. The beginning of the semester was always hard, especially in the fall. Most of the kids were more focused on their social lives than they were with class, and it was like pulling teeth to keep their attention.

Kristen Monroe.

Jesus.

He'd dealt with female students like her in the past. The whole professor and student fantasy was a popular one, and plenty of students had been smitten with him before.

But there was something about Kristen.

Fuck.

How he'd kept from staring at her in that short little skirt he wasn't sure. From the first moment she'd walked into his class, he'd definitely noticed her. She'd kept her eyes down the entire period the first day. When they finally made eye contact, he was practically dead in the water.

She was the most gorgeous student he'd ever seen by far. Her long, delicate legs and high, firm tits. He bit back a groan just thinking about her. A pang of guilt hammered his stomach. He was damn near old enough to be her father. When she'd bent over in front of his desk, his cock was so fucking hard it took everything he had not to snap the pen in his hand. He knew female students often found him attractive, and even some of the males.

He shook his head at himself in the mirror.

Get your shit together.

He couldn't afford to act on her obvious advances. Maybe she was just trying to get him back for giving her shit about being late the first day. She might lure him into a compromising position and threaten to get him fired. Use it as leverage. He'd dealt with plenty of devious students before who didn't like his rigid class-room structure or thought they could seduce their way into a passing grade.

There was no way he would fuck a student—especially one half his age. He had to push that idea far away. He was a man of authority, of power. There were serious ethical implications.

But still, the thought of her in the mini skirt walking through his classroom played through his mind on a loop. Grant shook his head, doing everything in his power to erase the memory. Trying to forget made it even worse. He swore he caught a glimpse of her white, cotton panties.

His jaw tensed. She knew exactly what she was doing.

What the hell was she doing?

What the hell was *he* doing?

He shouldn't have given the situation another thought, but there he was, making dinner and having some kind of cliché porn, role-playing fantasy. His mind went to places it shouldn't touch with a ten-foot pole, and to make matters worse, he didn't want it to stop. He imagined what he would to do her—what kind of noises she'd make when he bent her over his desk and fucked her from behind.

It was endless, how much he could teach her beyond the classroom.

Each thought quickly filled him with shame. He was the professor, and she was the student. The last thing he should've been thinking about was spanking her tight little ass while she squirmed on his knee.

No.

He could lose his job, his teaching credentials. It was a serious moral dilemma.

But fuck, the way her ass swayed in the skirt, and the way she blushed every time he glanced at her. He definitely loved a woman in a skirt, and even more so the way Kristen filled out hers.

Was she even a woman yet?

She probably wasn't older than twenty.

But then again, it wasn't like this was high school. She was easily past the age of consent, and he'd witnessed plenty of relationships between students and professors in the past.

Usually, nothing came of it, though they tried to keep it private. Maybe something could happen between them and never be spoken of again? Something brief and enjoyable?

But would it be enjoyable?

She was so young and innocent and he—wasn't.

If given the opportunity, he would do things to her she'd never experienced. He wouldn't be able to control himself, once put in that position.

"Fuck."

He looked down and noticed the chicken he'd been pan-frying was black on one side, and smoke rolled through the kitchen. He ran with the pan in his hand and dumped it in the sink.

He couldn't do this. He couldn't even think about it any longer.

Other teachers might fuck their students, but that wasn't him. It wasn't how he ran *his* classroom.

It didn't matter how attractive she was or how she looked at him. He was the professor, and that's exactly how it would stay.

———

Grant reached over and smacked the loud alarm clock. He lay there for a moment staring at the ceiling, then turned his gaze down to his rock-hard dick. He usually stuck to a tight schedule, going through his morning workout routine, taking his time with his coffee before he'd leave for class. Today was different. He hadn't slept well at all and felt it in every part of his body.

He glanced over at the clock and then back to his dick. His hand slowly glided down his stomach, and his eyes closed. He still smelled the perfume she'd worn to class a few days before, laced with a hint of body wash.

The sight of her bent over his desk played through his mind, and he stroked his cock, gently at first. The same way he would in real life, while he made her stand there, eagerly waiting for him.

He'd demand for her to stay still and tell her to offer him *his* pussy, however he instructed her to do so. His hand sped up on his dick as he thought about teasing her, tasting her. Fuck, her pussy tasted so sweet on his tongue as he went to his knees behind her and buried his face in her ass. He licked and sucked and bit, all the while noting every sound she made with each stroke of his tongue.

Then, he stood and asked her if she'd been well-behaved. She naturally shook her head, and he smacked her on the ass with a loud *thwack* that echoed through the classroom.

Her whole body tightened under his fingertips. That power, that control—*that* was what did it for him. His balls had already begun to tighten, and he thrust into Kristen's sweet, innocent pussy. It was like heaven in his mind—euphoric—tight, hot, wet, and snug. She jolted forward on the desk with his first thrust, and he took everything from her. Every innocent little look was his. He stood still with his arms behind his back and told her to fuck his cock, and to make it pleasing to him or he'd turn her ass red with his hand.

She bucked back against him, needy and helpless,

like she couldn't get enough of it. He enjoyed how hungry she was. She needed his cock like she needed air to breathe. She begged him to let her come, but he refused. The naughty little bitch had to know who was in control.

He stroked his cock furiously in the bed, gritting his teeth and grunting like a wild animal. He thought of all the different ways he could fuck her, and how he would angle his cock to hit all the perfect spots she probably hadn't yet discovered herself.

He was a professor. His job was to teach. And he would teach her how to come on his cock correctly, or she would be met with discipline. Finally, on the verge, he couldn't take it any longer. He gripped her hair and fucked multiple orgasms out of her, then came inside her smooth, slick cunt.

A groan echoed through his bedroom, and his toes curled as he filled Kristen Monroe with every last drop from his balls. Afterward, he shoved her to her knees, and allowed her to clean him with her tongue while she stared up at him with those helpless doe eyes.

He let out a large gasp, not realizing he'd been holding his breath. His chest rose and fell as he panted, and a fine sheen of sweat coated his body. Fucking hell, what was this girl doing to him?

His mind was a haze, and slowly the fog cleared and his wits returned. It wasn't how he'd planned to start his day, but he didn't mind. He was focused now.

Grant stared up at the ceiling and muttered, "Jesus Christ."

A rush of anxiety pounded into his stomach.

He didn't want to go to class again and see her after what he'd just done. But, there was another part of him that wanted to. What would she wear? What would she smell like? How would her voice sound? Had she just had a similar fantasy about him in the comfort of her own bed?

He pulled himself up and walked to the shower, stopping to look at his reflection along the way. Looking at his face, he knew what he had to do. He had to push her away, keep her at arm's length. If he got her alone, there was no telling what he would do.

He needed to be cold. Make it known through his actions that it would never happen, and if she wanted to pass his class, she would work hard and conduct herself properly.

He stepped into the shower and welcomed the hot water on his body.

When he got out, he gave himself another once over.

He knew he was attractive and kept himself in excellent shape. But shouldn't she be infatuated with the drunken frat boys on campus or the athletes? He wasn't arrogant about how he looked. But he flirted with enough women his own age to know he could turn heads.

Even though he'd just gotten out of bed, his hair still looked good, his beard didn't need to be trimmed, and his body was tight and toned from all the hard work he put into it.

But, he had to admit it was a pleasant surprise that a girl so young would be interested in him.

What was he doing? Critiquing himself over what some infatuated student thought of him? It was insane. He knew he'd have to tread carefully, or he'd wind up in trouble. He didn't know anything about this girl, save for what was shared with him through school records. There wasn't much there, either.

He didn't know what her home situation was like, where she came from, what she was trying to accomplish other than a degree in journalism. And what was she trying to get out of him?

She was a journalism major. Surely, she was capable of passing an introductory course on her own merits. Maybe it had nothing to do with being physically attracted to him or a passing grade. Maybe she had daddy issues or some sort of childhood trauma that prompted her to dress so slutty yesterday. Maybe it was attention-seeking. Maybe she just had a fetish for older men. Some girls experimented with other girls when they came to college. Maybe Kristen wanted to try her hand with a more experienced sexual partner.

His thoughts made more sense to him as he toweled off, but there were still too many unanswered questions. He couldn't reconcile some of them in his brain no matter how hard he tried.

Throughout his life, Grant hadn't had the best luck with women. There was something that wouldn't allow him to fully commit to the idea of one person for the rest of his life. There was a girl when he was young and foolish who'd almost changed that, but she chose another man at the last minute. It'd wrecked him for a long time and molded him into the man he was today.

He'd tried to act like it didn't matter, that he wasn't hurt by the situation, but he'd never considered committing to a woman after that. He'd resigned himself to the fact he would be alone for the rest of his life and decided to focus on his own career and happiness.

He wasn't old by any means, but compared to his students, he was practically ancient. And he was still old enough to feel like chasing random women was something he needed to give up. Maybe he could settle down with someone, if the right woman came along.

Despite his current thoughts, he was convinced the right one wouldn't be one of his students.

Even with the thoughts swirling through his mind, Grant couldn't help but notice he took extra care shaving the sides of his beard, and he wore a little more cologne than normal. He slicked his hair back over to the side of his head with some hair gel and took one final, critical look.

He stuck with the normal attire he wore every day— some things were too sacred to change. His suits were a wall he put up. They represented authority, the clear line between student and teacher. And that's how it would remain between himself and Kristen Monroe.

CHAPTER 4

The first week passed, and it soon became two weeks, then three, then the first month of school had come and gone. By now, most of the students had settled into their daily routine, and many of them had found their place in the school—socially and academically. There were those who practically lived in the study halls and library, and there were those who never went to class and partied all day, flunking class after class.

Although Kristen liked to believe she was one of the better students, she'd found herself drawn to the party lifestyle more than she wanted to admit. No matter how hard she tried, she fell further and further behind in class, and her grades reflected it.

It was to the point she was afraid to check online when grades were posted. Each time her overall average dropped more and more. She wasn't worried about losing scholarships or anything like that. Her parents paid for it, but she didn't want them to find out how poor she was doing. Not so much because of the money, that wouldn't matter to them, but she didn't want to disappoint them. She knew she had to make some changes to her lifestyle.

She'd call home all the time, but always avoided the topic of grades. It wasn't a conversation she wanted to have over the phone, and she knew there'd be some serious words exchanged when it happened.

"You're up early." Stefani stretched her arms over her head.

It was the first time all semester Kristen had been up before her. "Thought I'd get in some study time before class. I really need to pass this test, or I'm fucked." Kristen yawned. She reached forward and grabbed her book, not bothering to dress herself before she opened it to the page she needed.

"Why don't you ask someone for help?" Stefani was being tutored for two other classes.

"This shit is one of the easiest classes, and I can barely keep up." Kristen sighed and shook her head, staring at the page in front of her.

"Yeah, you didn't get off to a great start."

Kristen could hear a half-joking tone in Stefani's words, and she sighed. She hated the fact she'd been late on her first day. It felt like a curse.

"I was good at this stuff in high school. I don't know what happened. I don't even know where to look for a tutor." Kristen knew what happened, and so did Stefani, but neither would ever address the problem in a conversation. She'd partied and been lazy, and as a consequence, she fell behind. Now, it felt impossible to save her grades.

"Why don't you go talk to the professor?"

"What?" She didn't bother to mask the shocked tone in her voice.

Stefani stopped what she was doing and gave Kristen a strange look, and Kristen quickly angled her gaze back down to the book.

She'd told her she thought Professor Wiseman was hot, but she hadn't told her anything about the feelings she'd had for him—or what she wanted to do to him.

"It would be the logical first choice. Students can talk to professors, you know?"

"Yeah, yeah. I just—"

"Do you know another journalism professor or TA? It's normal to ask a professor for help."

Her eyes lingered on her friend for a few seconds, then she turned her attention to her breakfast. She hadn't considered it, but now that the possibility was in front of her, butterflies swarmed into the pit of her stomach. What would she say to him?

It would be embarrassing. Over the course of the month, she'd done everything she could to flirt with him without it being obvious, and he'd been nothing but rude to her.

Still, she'd noticed, after the first day, he looked perfectly put together every morning after that. The few occasions she'd seen him at other times on campus, he wasn't dressed nearly as sharp. She could've sworn he was doing it because of her.

"I don't know. The whole class is subjective. I don't want him to fail me if I ask for help. He'll know I've been behind." Kristen kept her head down as she spoke. She didn't want Stef to be able to read her expressions and figure out the real issue she faced. She wasn't worried about him failing her. She just didn't want him to think she was stupid. Which wasn't true at all. She retained every word he'd spoken and the way he'd said it.

Sure, she might have daydreamed about what she wanted him to do to her too, but that was different. She made an effort to learn everything she could. She wanted to impress him. She'd fallen behind on her assignments because she didn't want to turn in subpar work. She'd only turned in one in the beginning, and the result had been horrible. She hadn't given him anything since.

She had zero confidence in the test she was about to take. No matter what she did, it wouldn't be good enough.

She was convinced she was going to bomb.

————

"Anyone have questions?" Professor Wiseman glanced around the classroom with raised eyebrows as he spoke. He had a way of simultaneously staring at everyone and no one. Every time he did it, Kristen pretended they were the only two people in the room. That his gaze was intently fixed on her, but her eyes always dropped if he lingered in her direction.

"Nobody? Okay then, class is dismissed. Don't forget

about the test coming up Friday." Professor Wiseman spoke loud enough that his voice carried over the din created as students gathered their things and prepared to leave the class. Kristen's heart kicked into overdrive, pounding in her chest, and a lump formed in her throat. She wiped her sweaty palms down her skirt.

She'd decided to ask for help, but she couldn't think of the right thing to say. How would she open the conversation? What would he say back to her? So many thoughts whirled through her brain that it went blank.

As she walked up to his desk, the smell of his cologne landed in her nose, and she just wanted to breathe him in. A sudden wave of adrenaline coursed through her limbs when he looked up at her with his cold, blue eyes sitting behind his glasses.

"Something I can help you with?" He looked up at her. His words were harsh and uninviting, and his tone suggested no bullshit.

Why was he so mean to her?

The knot in her throat swelled. "Y-yes."

Her hand trembled when she held out the one assignment she'd turned in. She quickly sat it on the desk in front of him, trying to hide her shaky fingers. Despite being nervous, she walked around his desk so she could stand next to him. He was like a magnet, the force yanking her closer, despite the fact her brain screamed for her to keep a safe distance.

A vein popped out on his neck, and she could practically feel his heartbeat on it as she neared. His entire body tensed for a quick second, and his hands balled into fists before returning to a relaxed state.

I'm making him nervous too.

Calm washed over her, and her anxiety melted away, knowing she affected him the same way he did her.

Kristen leaned over his desk and pointed at a few sentences she remembered working hard on but was still ashamed to admit were her own.

"I don't understand the grading on these."

He glanced over at her and gulped. His eyes darted back to the paper. "What do you not understand?"

He was back to using his asshole tone. What was his deal? If he liked her, why was he being a dick? Two could play at this game.

"Everything. I worked *hard* on those. Is it my *form?*" She arched her back and stretched like a cat, as if she were sore and needed a massage. Kristen grinned on the inside, knowing the words would stir him even more.

He tried to control himself, but she noticed every little detail about him. His breathing sped up, and she wondered if his heart beat in his chest as hard as hers.

She pointed at a semi-colon on the page and breathed him in once more. Her pussy was already wet just because of the close proximity. She could easily grab him by his hair and pull his head down to where she needed it. Her clit swelled and throbbed just at the sound of him breathing. Goosebumps pebbled along the backs of her arms thinking about his rough fingers digging into her hips.

Her eyes followed from the paper up to his face where he studied what she'd written.

He didn't say anything for a few moments, then handed her the paper.

"It's not terrible. Just not great."

She stood there, staring nervously.

He sighed. "What would you like me to do? You've only turned in one assignment. Maybe you're not putting forth enough effort."

She should've felt embarrassed at what he'd said, but all she could think was that he'd paid enough attention to realize she'd only turned in one paper. The class was huge. There was no way he could keep track of everyone personally, but he had for her.

Her hands were clammy once more. Why was it so hard to just fucking breathe around him? And he'd asked her a simple question that heated her up even more.

"What would you like me to do?"

Everything. Do anything you want to me.

She wasn't sure how to actually answer. Her brain was nothing but a giant mass of exposed wires.

"Umm, is there—I mean, maybe you know a tutor?"

He let out another exasperated sigh. "Well, did you go to student services?"

"No."

"You're aware there's a department for helping out with problems like these, right?" He glanced up at her and seared her with those eyes. "So that you don't bother your professor with it."

Of course, she knew that. But she didn't want to go to student services. She wanted to be in the room with him. She wanted any opportunity she could get to ask him questions.

"S-sorry. I didn't know."

He smirked as if to say, *we both know damn well what's happening here.*

She rose and smoothed down the front of her skirt.

She caught his eyes glancing to her legs and then back up to her face as quickly as possible.

God, there was something about this man that made her ramble like an idiot. Part of her worried he'd think of her as some kind of helpless airhead.

They both sat there, staring at one another for a few seconds that seemed like an eternity. His eyes raked up and down her body, this time without any attempts to avert his stare.

His gaze moved up to her face, still perfectly framed in his hot-as-all-fuck glasses. He let out a breathy sigh. "I normally don't do this. But I can help you with a few things."

Houston, we have lift off.

A wave of delicious tension swam through her body and funneled straight down into her pussy. It was like floating on air. Everything became bright and more radiant. Colors were vivid.

"You would do that?" She blinked. "For me?" Her face had to be pink with excitement.

He smiled. Not a warm, happy smile. It was more like a devilish grin. But it was still the first time he'd ever smiled at her. "Stop by after class tomorrow. We can go over a few things."

She nodded, unable to even think of classes she had the next day. It didn't matter. She would clear her schedule for him.

"Thank you. I *really* appreciate this." She
away as fast as she could.

What had she just done? What had *he* just done?

It had to be nothing. He was just being nice, showing
her some kind of mercy. But the way his eyes seared into
her flesh and warmed her all over. The tone of his voice.
She hadn't seen this coming at all, him offering to help
her personally.

"I expect you to work, Miss Monroe."

She whipped back around to face him.

His face was tense, and his eyes narrowed. "Do *not*
waste my time."

She nodded. "I promise."

She turned on her heel and pushed through
the door.

Holy fuck, he was so intense. And she was going to
be given time with him, alone.

She had him entirely to herself.

The thought ran through her mind once more.

Alone. Tomorrow.

To continue reading Professor's Pet visit

amazon.com

ABOUT THE AUTHOR

Alex hails from the Midwest and currently resides in
New Orleans.
He enjoys writing steamy romance but more
importantly he enjoys the "research" required to
produce the steamy scenes. If you like filthy-mouthed,
possessive alpha heroes and steamy romance, then he's
the author for you!

Sign up for my newsletter and receive EXCLUSIVE
content throughout the year
subscribepage.com/alex-wolf

Where you can follow me